RAINBOWS EVER AFTER

A Black Rainbow Happily Ever After Novella

J.J. McAvoy

Rainbows Ever After
Copyright © 2017 by J.J. McAvoy
ISBN-13: 978-1544011905
ISBN-10: 1544011903

NYLA Publishing
350 7th Avenue, Suite 2003, NY 10001, New York.
http://www.nyliterary.com

Dedication

For everyone who never wants the happily ever to end…

PART ONE

BABY: DAY 1

LEVI

The world was full of liars. I was sure of it. It had to be. I was sure of it. Throughout my life, I've had to endure many people shoving their kids in my face, saying how they were so cute. How there was no other kid on the planet as beautiful as their child. I'd awkwardly just agree, smile, give the kid a little nod, and move on. But now as I held my child—my son— cute wasn't good enough; beautiful was just the bare minimum, barely cutting it. Ulric was pulchritudinous. Yes, pulchritudinous, a 15-letter, 5-syllable word that meant a person of such breathtaking and heartbreaking beauty effort needed to be used in order to say it. Closing my eyes and opening them again, I smiled wider seeing him sleeping soundly in my arms. He was actually the cutest baby in the world, and as such, everyone else was a bunch of liars.

"Shh…" I whispered softly as he started to twist and turn in my arms. His light face bunched up as he prepared to demand his next feeding. I didn't want to wake her, but—

"Someone's hungry," she said softly, her head tilted at us in the chair beside her. She smiled and opened her arms for him. Standing up with him, I moved to the side of her bed, gently snuggling him into her beautiful brown arms. He was already a genius; the moment he was with her, he knew food was coming, calmed down, and turned toward her breast, leaning over I helped open her gown enough.

"Ahh…"

"Does it hurt?" I asked, watching her carefully.

She giggled and shook her head smiling down at him. "No, it just kind of feels like a tiny vacuum getting attached to me."

"Do you need anything?" I asked, stroking the side of her dark hair. She shook her head no, unable to look away from him. I understood the feeling.

That's how pulchritudinous he was. He could steal the attention of the love of my life, and I'd gladly accept it because … because my heart felt like it was about to burst out of my chest.

Feeling my phone vibrate, I pulled it out to see the stream of texts pouring in from both of our families.

"Are they really trying to get here at this hour?" Thea asked, finally looking up at me.

"As they should be," I nodded, texting my mother back. "What is a New Year's celebration compared to him?"

"Can't believe you held out for the new year," she said to him.

"I can't believe you did either," I teased, grinning, remembering how much she'd jiggled, wiggled, and begged for him to come out.

"Shut up."

"Shh…" I reached over, putting my fingers over his tiny ears. "Don't teach him bad words yet. You know I'm going to fu—screw up with that later."

She rolled her brown eyes at me. "You're ridiculous."

"I'm happy," I told her, kissing her forehead. "thank you…thank you for all the ways you've blessed my life."

She swallowed, nodding, fighting the tears in her eyes. I was too.

Was it possible to explode from too much happiness? If so, I was sure I was ready to simultaneously combust. The only thing stopping me was my fear that I wouldn't get to stare at them more.

God…these really were the best years of my life. Even on the worst days, it was the best.

THEA

He wasn't playing fair.

But, then again, he never played fair. He just said whatever he wanted, without hesitation, smothering me with all of it, and it hurt in the best kind of way. Even now as I was struggling to concentrate, both of us completely exhausted, his dark hair a mess on his head, his green eyes fighting off sleep, he made it hard for me not to stare at him. If he was this happy, what did that make me?

I never figured this would be my life and yet here I was. Here we all were. Sitting in a hospital bed on New Year's Day, now, fireworks and cheering still lingering on outside even though it had been hours since midnight. It was like it was all one big celebration for him. Our son. I was a mother. I was someone's love, fiancée, and I'd soon be a wife. I was blissful. But the truth was we'd both been over the moon since I told him.

Looking back, even on the days we'd been annoyed with each other, we were content.

"We did good, Levi," I nodded to him as he gently poked Ulric's cheek. He looked like a kid himself, so in awe, and curious.

"Damn right we did." He smirked, and then frowned at himself. "His first word is going to be a swear word, isn't it?"

I laughed, and Ulric lifted his hand up like he was trying to reach for me, to touch my voice. Or maybe that was just my mommy brain, he could have been telling us to keep it down he was eating here.

"I'm glad it's just us for now." He bent down and kissed our son's head.

"So am I." We wouldn't have minded if all of our family was here, we were sure they'd be here soon, but having these couple of moments to ourselves with him was everything we could have wanted.

"I love you." It was only a fraction of what I wanted to say.

"Love me enough to stop making me go out at two a.m. for Korean food?"

"Let's not get crazy here." I grinned, and he sighed, allowing Ulric to grab his finger.

"At least she can't blame you anymore," he said to our son.

I'd put him through the wringer while I was pregnant. I knew that. So did he. But looking back, at least we had some funny memories. My mind replayed them all like a movie reel, and I couldn't wait for Denise, Levi's mother, to get here because I finally understood what she meant.

"My dad told me it would be like this." Levi brushed his hand over Ulric's head again. "He has never been more right."

I wanted to ask him to elaborate, but I felt like it was personal. Kind of like the talks I'd had with his mother.

"Welcome to the world, Ulric Black," I said down to him when he was done. "We've been waiting for you since we found out you were coming."

"I've wanted him since I met you," Levi said, looking up at me with those stunning green eyes of his, which tonight looked evening more striking due to the shine in them. "Since that first week, I've wanted you to be the mother of my children, and I've wanted him. I love you, Thea. And I love him."

There he was, being unfair again.

PREGNANCY: MONTH 1

THEA

"Twelve hours? You were in labor for twelve hours?"

"Bethan was fifteen."

I groaned, looking down at my own flat stomach. "Don't you dare."

Denise laughed at me. "Yeah, but don't rush too much, though. Enjoy it. With Levi, I always wanted him to be close by, calling me *Mommy*. One day it changed to *Mom*, and the next thing I know, he's an adult who's going to be a father. Being a mom is like that. You want your kids to be independent and grow up healthy and happy. But you also want them to need you. Even when they're adults."

"Levi talks about you guys all the time." I felt like hugging her, and I wasn't sure why. "He tells me all the fun things he did as a kid. In all honestly, I'm jealous. I wish that it was like that for me."

"The good thing about not having the best childhood is you know exactly what to do to make sure that your kids do."

I hadn't thought about it that way. I—Levi and I—would now be responsible for another person's life, to make sure he or she didn't end up a black rainbow, stripped of colors.

"Thea?"

"Huh?" I snapped, reaching to take the spoons from her. "Sorry, it just kinda hit me again. There is a person growing in me."

"Freaky, but cool, right?" She smirked, just like Levi did when he guessed what was on my mind.

"Exactly," I replied as I saw her moving to take the plates. "Oh, I got it!" I tried to take them back from her, but Denise was too quick and had already grabbed all the plates and silverware, and moved to the kitchen, much faster than any other sixty-year-old woman in heels I'd ever seen.

"The food was amazing; you're a much better cook than I was at your age." She smiled, placing the dishes in the sink and rolling up the sleeves of her two-hundred-dollar cardigan. "I'm so happy, I have to put it to use. After his divorce, I worried he'd just be *Levi Black*, the amazing lawyer." I liked how even she called him the amazing lawyer. Though I knew she was teasing a little bit. "Then you came. And now our family has gotten bigger and much brighter. I want you to know I'm grateful. And I want you to also forgive me in the future because I'm really going to spoil the heck out of that kid."

She pointed to my stomach and sounded so excited. I laughed.

"I can see it now. This kid is going to have coats in ten different colors with matching shoes and hats."

"And gloves, and scarves, and tiny dresses or suits." She was giddy, which was making me giddy. "And that's just the first year. The moment he starts getting older, you'll see Walter riding up on different sized bikes."

"Oh gosh." I remembered Bethan, with her room of dresses, and I imagined needing a larger place soon.

"I want you to know, you're my daughter, too, Thea. So that means I'm going to invite you for lunches and shopping, and to get our hair and nails and anything else done that I can think of. You're important to us, too. So even if Levi tries hogging you, you will have tell him to sit in the corner to hang out while you are spending time with his old, attention-begging mother."

My throat went dry, and I couldn't bring myself to look at her for a moment, only nodding and folding the towel in my hands. "I ... thank you, Denise."

"I'll accept that for now..." She hugged me. "But let's work up to *Mom*, okay?"

I hadn't had a mom; my actual mother didn't feel like my mother. And so this ... this was special for me. "Yes ... Mom."

"Perfect." She squeezed tighter.

LEVI

When I didn't hear water, or them muttering back and forth again, I glanced over my shoulder. I wasn't sure what I expected, but seeing them embrace was what I'd hoped for and gotten.

"You're getting your ass kicked." I looked back to my father as he stared down at the chess match in front us, his eyes unwavering. He took my knight and then looked back up at me. "I fear for your clients."

"My clients are fine, thank you." My jaw cracked to the side as I looked at the hole I'd fallen into … wait. Relaxing my face, I glanced back to him. "Really, Dad? You've resorted to cheating now?"

"Cheating?" He huffed angrily. "You rude little—"

I reached down and rearranged the pieces. "This was the last move I made so how in the heck did my rook move all the way over there?"

"I pray you have a son who's exactly like you," he muttered, leaning back in his seat. I chuckled and glanced over my shoulder once before pulling out the flask near the arm of the chair. He glanced back to them before he slid his cup of cranberry juice closer.

"My boy." He nodded proudly.

"Oh, now you're happy to have a son like me." I snickered, adding some to my juice before hiding it again.

"I never said weren't both a joy and a frustration." He tipped his glass.

"Levi Roman Black!" My mother called. I jumped before the glass got to my lips. "Did you spike your father's drink?"

How? How did she know?

I looked to my father who made it worse by chugging the evidence.

"What drink?" I asked her trying to be his lawyer. "There is no more drink, and as such, there is nothing spiked."

She marched over and even my father sat up straighter.

"It was just one—"

"Just one glass. You know with your heart condition that you shouldn't be drinking even drop."

"You already have me eating grass three times a week—"

She snapped her fingers at me, and I stared at them for a moment. Then back at her. Sighing, I handed her the flask. But she wasn't done there. She took my glass too.

"He's the one with the condition!"

"Are you the prosecutor or the defense?" my father muttered.

"And you're the one who takes after him, so you're welcome in advance," she replied.

My mouth dropped open, preparing to say something, but my father shook his head, but I went forward to my death anyway. "At least let me finish the glass. Dad drank his." If I was throwing him under the bus, I might as well drag him a little too.

She paused, turned back to me, and I froze, recognizing that look. She rejoined Thea, who was trying her best not to laugh at me.

"Thea, dear, don't you think it's a little unfair that you can't drink for nine whole months while you carry your soon-to-be husband's child?"

Karma had no grace period. Just as I'd thrown my father under the bus, so had she done to me.

"Absolutely!" Thea said passionately. And just as I'd dragged my father, she decided to rub it in. "I'm also barefoot and pregnant in the kitchen while he's just having a grand ol' time."

Why couldn't I keep my mouth shut?

"I lied actually," my mother continued as she poured my glass and flask down the drain. "It's actually much longer than nine months … breast feeding time, too."

"Really?" Thea pouted.

"Don't worry. You have a whole support team, right, Levi?" There it was—the final nail in my coffin.

I looked to my father who just nodded like he knew it was coming.

"Levi?" Thea called.

Closing my eyes, I forced myself to smile. "Sure."

Nine months plus without alcohol?

"The first eight months are the hardest," my father said softly, reaching for his chess piece again. "After that, you get so busy preparing and panicking that you're too scared to drink."

"She did this to you too?"

"Twice," he said, and it sounded just as painful as I thought. "You got off easy. I'd gone out to drink with a few buddies at the firm, and she was so upset. Irrationally upset, was what I told her. But she told me if I drank again without her, she'd raise you on her own."

I took his pawn and asked, "How did she even know?"

"Don't ask questions, son. The answers will scare you. They pick up." He shook his head, and for some reason, the thought made me laugh. "What? I'm being serious."

"I know. I was just thinking how I want a son. Just so I could say those types of lines to him." I laughed again … I couldn't stop laughing. I was going to be a father. Me.

"Yes, half the time he'll ignore you," he added, obviously distracted as he searched the board for a victory.

"And the other half?"

He paused and looked up at me with familiar green eyes. "The other half he'll end up being much wiser than you. And you'll be so shocked and amazed at the person he's become you'll end up letting yourself lose chess games just to spend time with him."

The corner of my lip creeped up. "So you let yourself lose now, *Grandpapa*?"

"Yes, and you're not getting any other explanation from me either, *Dad*," he said proudly, sitting back in his chair, not making his final move into my trap.

I took a deep breath and sat back as well. "I always knew that one day I wanted to be a father. I just didn't realize that one day was finally here."

"Now everything starts."

"What?"

"Falling in love. Getting married. That's all the prequel. Actually starting a family … seeing that family grow … that's the movie and goes by quicker than you think. That's when you feel love is bottomless."

"There are those lines again." I tried to tease, but in all honestly I wanted to know what it was he was trying to explain.

"I stole them from my father," he admitted. "I told you he was a writer, didn't I?"

"Then you have no problem letting me steal them?"

"*My* father was a writer," he repeated. "*Your* father is a lawyer and rightfully had them copyrighted," he said, jokingly.

Rolling my eyes, I shook my head. This was one of the reasons I devoted myself to winning arguments … to undo the years of trauma losing to this man. I hoped I was half as great as my father. I hoped Thea and I were even greater parents.

THEA

Something was off.

I stood there for almost two full minutes, watching as he sat on our bed, his thick framed reading glasses on his nose, dressed in only his dark blue pajama bottoms, his bare muscular chest tempting me.

"Levi?"

"Huh?" he asked, his head turning toward me, but his eyes still on the computer screen. When I didn't say anything, he glanced over, and once he looked, he couldn't look away.

"*Jesus…*" he whispered, reaching up to take off his glasses. His gaze traveled my legs until he stopped right at the small silk robe, which didn't even cover my ass, showing the black lace of my panties. "You're way too far away."

"Don't mind me. Just keep staring at the computer. I'll go change into something more—"

"Oh, no you don't." He tossed his laptop to the end of the bed and rushed over to me. Grabbing my arm before I could go back into the bathroom, he pinned me against the door. "I've been waiting to be alone with you all day."

"Really, and that's why you were—"

"Why I got excited and nervous and curious, so I was Googling what happens now … now that you're … we're pregnant." He couldn't even say it with a straight face. He just kept grinning at me.

Looking down, I pulled the robe open so he could see my bra. He started laughing, which made me laugh too.

"This was my plan. I was going to tell you right before I got annoyed and asked you in the shower," I said to him as he stared at my black, bedazzled bra with the words *I'm pregnant* written on the cups.

Calming down, he stood straighter, placing his hands on my cheeks. He just kept staring at me.

"What? Why are you staring at me like that?"

"You're pregnant."

"I am."

"You said yes."

"I did."

"You love me."

"I do."

"How can I not stare at you like this?" he said softly, resting his forehead against mine. "This is my how-the-hell-did-I-get-so-lucky-to-get-everything-I-ever-wanted stare?"

Taking his hand, I led him to the bed, pushed him onto his back, and straddled his waist. He sat up on his elbows, his brows raised, grinning at me. Staring down at him, I softly brushed my thumb across his bottom lip, before running my finger down the center of his chest, around his pecs, and down to his abs. He closed his eyes, his breathing slowed, and he relaxed under me. Leaning over, I kissed him. He opened his mouth, but I just kissed the side, then his chin, his light stubble not at all bothering me; in fact, it turned me on more. Kissing my way to his ear, I gently bit his earlobe.

I wanted to tell him just how much I loved him too. The words couldn't come, so I just kept kissing him. Kissing down his neck.

"Ah…" he moaned, holding my waist, which only made it easier for me to grind myself on him.

Sitting up, I reached behind my back to undo my bra hooks and threw it to the side. The moment he saw my breasts, he reached for them, his cold hands making me jump. He squeezed, sitting up, running his thumb over my nipple before taking it into his mouth. His arm wrapped around my waist as he kissed and sucked on me.

"Oh…" I licked my lips, trying to focus, but he was relentless, alternating from one breast to the other his tongue running over my nipple over and over again before he took me into his mouth.

I felt myself getting hotter as he got harder beneath me. Putting my hands on his shoulders, I pushed him onto his back again. He exhaled deeply from his nose, frustrated, lust blazing in his green eyes.

With my face just above his, I grabbed his chin and said, "Behave, Mr. Black."

He extended just enough to kiss my lips. "Make me, Future Mrs. Black."

When he got like this, nothing but a rough fuck could calm him back down. Reaching into his pajamas, I grabbed hold of his hot cock and squeezed. He bared his teeth, jerking forward in my hands.

"You play dirty."

"You're the one who taught me how," I reminded him, kissing his chin as I stroked him. My bare breasts pressed against his chest. His head bent back, allowing me to continue where I'd originally left off—his neck—sucking until a small, red mark appeared.

"Baby..." He exhaled, his mouth open. "I have ... court ... in the morning."

"So?" I squeezed his cock, sucking and licking and kissing his neck again.

"I can't ... I can't ... I can't have hickies..."

"Thank God for scarves."

"It's ... May."

"Poor you." I smirked and ran my tongue down his chest, then bit him.

"Damn you!" he cried out.

"No, baby," I said softly, sliding down to kiss his abs until I got to the waistband of his pajama pants. "Is that any way to talk to the mother of your child?" His dick was so hard, it stood proudly when I pulled it from inside his pants.

Licking the tip of him before sliding my tongue down him until I'd gotten to his balls, wanting to take them into my mouth when he grabbed on to my head and pulled me up and then flipped me over. He pinned my hands over my head.

"You shouldn't have said that last part," he whispered, his eyes on my lips. "You had your fun ... now I'm going to have mine."

He stood up. Taking off his bottoms, he walked to the dresser, as my heart thumped against my chest. When he came back, his cock was pointed directly at me, and he flipped the top of the oil with his thumb.

"Turn over," he demanded, but I couldn't. I didn't want to look away from him. He was giving me chills. "Now, Thea."

Doing as commanded, I turned on to my stomach, feeling the bed shift when he got back on. He gently he took my hair and pulled it into a ponytail, brushing his fingers over my shoulder.

"Levi..."

"Shh," he whispered directly into my ear, sending another shiver down my spine. Trembling eagerly, I closed my eyes, just as I felt the oil drip onto my back, and then just slide down me. He didn't care that it poured on to the sheets either. He grabbed my ass, squeezing and rubbing making sure the oil slid between my cheeks before throwing the bottle to the side. From my waist, he rubbed up my back.

"Ohh..." The more he rubbed, the warmer the oil got. But it wasn't just that ... it tingled. Biting on my finger as he reached under massaging my breasts, his cock sliding between my ass cheeks creating that same fire again. "Ahh..."

What was this? It felt so good … and so damn frustrating at the same time. Feeling his hard cock against my ass was driving me insane. Grabbing on to the sheets, now sweating, panting, one of his hands moved to grip my neck. With the other to my ass, he pressed himself down on me again.

"Please," I whispered, my gaze unable to focus.

"We're just getting started baby," he whispered back, biting the top of my ear, his grip on my neck still tight, my breathing slowing down, making everything else feel like it was slowing down with it.

What else could he do? His hand was at my pussy, stroking me.

"I need you," I begged. "Please … oh…"

He stuck two of his fingers into me, pulling them out so slowly I was ready to cry.

"You're so wet, baby," he said as he tortured me.

"Damn you."

"Is that any way to speak to the father of your child?" He had the nerve to snicker.

"You—Oh … oh…" I pulled on the sheets so tightly, I was sure my nails had ripped through as he slowly entered my ass.

"What were you saying?" he asked, completely inside me, but giving me no time to respond. I rose on to all fours. As he gently stretched me out, pulling out some and thrusting back in, he played with my clit. I reminded myself that I'd planned to be charge tonight, and somehow I was at his mercy. Pushing myself off the bed, and sitting up on my knees, I reached back and wrapped my arm around his neck.

"I…" I closed my eyes for a second as his pace quickened. "I was … saying … your…"

He bent over, his lips over my own before I could get the words out … not that I was making much progress anyway. This kiss was much more lustful—sloppy. He held on to me, ramming himself deeper, and faster—so hard that we both fell on to our sides. Our lips broke apart as our moans filled the room. Even then he didn't let go, and I didn't want him to. My whole body trembled.

"Oh my…" I gasped.

"Thea … ah," he said as he finished, kissing my shoulder.

"You just couldn't let me run tonight, could you?" I whispered, rolling over to see him.

His eyes were closed but the corner of his lip turned up. "Blame yourself for being so beautiful."

Rolling my eyes, I tried to get up, but he held on to me.

"I'm sticky."

"Stick to me then," he muttered, wrapping both of his arms around me.

"How do you always have the perfect comeback?"

He grinned not answering but gathering me into his arms.

BABY: DAY 1

LEVI

"The cavalry has arrived," I said, sitting up from the bed as she gently pulled on Ulric's hat. I paused, taking out my phone to take another picture.

"Levi." She made a face at me. "That's like your hundredth photo."

"Hundred and one, but who's counting," I said, taking another one.

She rolled her eyes at me. "Go get everyone."

"They can wait; look, he moved his nose!" I pointed, and her head snapped down to see as I took another photo.

She shook her head, and looked at me. "We've become 'those people,' Levi."

"What people?"

"Those people with thousands of photos of their kids, who get super excited when their kid has gas."

I snickered and put my phone back in my pocket. "Everyone wants to be those people, but they just don't know it."

"Oh my gosh, your daddy is cuckoo," she said to our son who'd been in and out of sleep for the last couple of hours. Who knew watching someone, a child, our child, sleep would be so exciting?

"Knock knock," a very familiar voice called from behind the door just before my sister, Bethan, now a blonde, poked her head inside. The moment she saw the baby, she gasped and invited herself all the way in, dressed in a long, one-shoulder black gown.

"He's beautiful, Thea." She gasped hovering over them.

"I had something to do with that, too," I said, but she just waved me off, cooing at the baby. But her and Thea were laughing again.

"Don't take it personally," Tristan muttered, entering the room next, in his black tux, Bellamy asleep in his arms, the bottom her puffy gold dress sticking out under his arm. "She's upset with me and has decided to take it out on the whole male sex."

He sighed tiredly before his brown eyes shifted, and the corner of his lips turned up. "I'd shake your hand, but father duties." He lifted Bellamy a little in his arms. "He looks like a future heartbreaker."

"With parents like us, how could he not be?" I said softly, looking at how big Bellamy was already. Three years old, soon to be four. "Do you want me call for a small bed for her?"

"Never, and Happy New Year," he replied, moving over to say hello to Thea and Ulric. Bethan placed her hand on his Ulric's head, smiling up to him, and they shared a look. Whatever fight they were having, or had, was apparently a moot point.

"Oh..." I turned to see my mother, dressed in a champagne gown, her hair pinned up. She stepped inside, with her hand over her mouth.

"I'd like to hold him sometime today, Denise," my father said to her, and she smacked his arm.

He gave me a handshake, which led to a hug. "Congratulations, son."

"Thank you, Dad." I exhaled patting his back as he patted my own.

"He's ... oh ... he's perfect." My mother cried as she held him in her arms. "Walter, come and see."

You didn't have to tell him twice. He walked over to them, putting his hand on Thea's cheek as she laid back on the pillows, before he turned to my mother and son. "Look at those cheeks. Just like when Levi was born," he whispered down to Ulric.

I'd just taken a step to them when there was a knock at the door again and and in walked Thea's little sister, Selene, and her father, Benjamin, still bundled up. Selene gave me a huge hug, and had you know her three years ago, you'd never realize this was the same person.

"I would say 'way to go,' but my sister kinda did all the hard work..." she teased and I pitched her side making her jump. "Just kidding ... but not really." She ran away from me, and toward her sister before I could get her again. "Sis, you finally look like the mom you are."

"Oh, you are so lucky I'm on painkillers or I'd kick you," Thea grumbled, but still accepted the hug.

"Ben?" I looked back to him when he hadn't moved.

He blinked, coming out of whatever deep thought he'd lost himself in. Putting his hand on my shoulder, he gave it a good squeeze. Nothing else needed to be said; I understood from the look on his face, as he headed over to his daughter.

"Hi, Daddy," she said to him.

"Hi, Thea bear." He kissed her forehead. "You did good."

My mother moved, lifting Ulric for Ben to hold. But he just froze. My mother, never one to be ignored, took his arms and carefully put Ulric in them, still supporting his head until he did it himself.

"Thea, you sure he's yours? He so calm." He laughed, his eyes glistening with tears. "Your mother screamed her pretty little head off when I first held her."

"He's hers all right. The little guy had no patience, so that's proof enough," I said, moving to take a seat beside her.

"Mom," Thea said sleepily, and my mother went to her. "Make them stop picking on me. I'm too tired to fight back."

She laughed and sat on the opposite side of her. "Next person to tease my daughter while she's defenseless will get a shoe to the skull ... good enough?" She directed that last part to Thea, who gave her a thumbs up.

"So what did you name him?" Bethan asked, now sitting Tristan's lap, and Bellamy in hers.

"Ulric," Thea and I said together.

Selene and Ben both smiled, obviously knowing why, but the rest of my family was a little confused.

"It was my grandfather's name," Thea said proudly.

"Ulric Black," my father repeated.

"Ulric Pierre Black," I corrected, looking at my mother as she held Thea's hand.

"I'm guessing Ulric Oidhche Black didn't have the same ring." My father pouted, and my mother groaned.

"Oidhche?" Selene asked, trying not to laugh.

"Levi's grandfather, on his father's side, was Oidhche Black, and to this day, Walter still believes I should have named Levi that." My mother shook her head.

Bethan laughed. "Oh, that would have been awesome! Why did you strip me years' worth of puns?"

"Hey!" my father said to her. "It means 'the night' in Scottish."

"Night-Black," Thea, said nodding her head. "That's kinda cool."

"Don't—"

"Ulric Pierre-Oidhche Black," she cut me off already going there.

"What … is he a prince? Why does he need four names?" I asked her.

"Because it sounds cool, right?" She looked to my father, who was halfway to the moon.

"She's the smart one." My father nodded, now holding Ulric. "Listen to her."

Thea looked up to me, hopeful, and I lost the fight the moment she'd said it out loud. "Ulric Pierre-Oidhche Black, it is."

"In honor of the little prince, and everyone looking so *dapper*, let's take a picture. It is a new year, after all," Selene said, taking out her phone.

"We should see if a nurse can take the photo—" Ben said, but Selene just shook her head. Reaching into her coat and she pulled out what she needed.

"What are selfie sticks for if not for group selfies?" she replied.

"On three, everyone say, 'Oidhche.'"

Both my mother and I groaned.

THEA

"Umm…" I yawned tilting my head to see Levi resting with his left hand resting on Ulric's tiny bed foot. It was just the three of us again. Everyone else left once the snow fall got heavier. By the time they called us to let us know they were home, the snow had come down even heavier. The doctors told us to stay until the blizzard was over. We were fine but the cold weather and the road conditions on top of it still beginning new year's, it was just safer. I wasn't going to risk it with lunatics driving or the black ice.

I'm such a mom.

I grinned, looking at Ulric, watching his tiny chest rise and fall as he slept peacefully alongside his father. I felt bad; it didn't too look comfortable for Levi.

Nnmmmm

Nmmmm

Levi's phone vibrated on the bed next to my leg. I picked it up, thinking it was his mother, but it was none other than the twin clowns. Dialing instead of texting, it was only a second before I saw their faces.

"Atticus, Viv, happy new year." I waved at them.

"Look at her." Atticus grinned, completely bundled up as he walked outside, the street lamps on in the background. "While someone of us were getting drunk and kissing strangers, Thea Cunning was bringing life into the world, all while looking like a model."

"What can I say? I'm awesome. You know this," I replied dusting off my shoulder.

"Where is he?" Viviane jumped into the frame, snow in her dark hair and on her bronze cheeks, apparently totally uninterested in me.

"Hi, Viv, happy New Year! How's the weather? Oh you look—""

"Yes. Yes. Hi, Thea. Happy New Year. It's tits up cold out, and if this person had anything more than Hot Pockets and beer in his refrigerator I wouldn't know that … so where is the child?"

Grumpy, as always. I made a face, sticking out my bottom lip, turning the camera around so they could see, I heard them gasp and *aww*, which made me all teary again; damn hormones apparently didn't exit with him.

"Don't we make a good kid?" I raised my chin a little higher in pride, once I turned the camera back around.

"I hate adding to your ego … but yeah. He's so cute, Thea," Viviane replied.

"How does it feel to be a mom?" Atticus asked.

"I don't know, it hasn't hit me yet," I whispered.

"Thea, we'll call you back when Mother Nature isn't trying to bury us under a mountain of snow," she said, and just like that the connection was lost. A few congratulatory texts poured in from all the people at his law firm.

I looked toward the window, but couldn't see out. Lifting the sheets, I tried to move my legs, but they were asleep.

"Where are you going?" Levi yawned sitting up from his chair cracking his head side to side. He glanced down at Ulric to make sure he was alright before looking to me again.

"To see what it's like outside, and use the bathroom … actually the bathroom first," I said, trying to push myself off the bed. He came around to my side to help me stand. "Levi, it's—"

"All I've done is take pictures, watched you both, so let me help with this," he said, and I was sure he would have carried me if the doctors hadn't said walking was good for me. He held his arm around my waist and only because he was there and warm, I leaned into him more.

"Oh, bag." I pointed to our baby bag, which I was still surprised he'd remembered. He loosened up and I held on to the bathroom door. "I just need my toilet bag."

"The green one, right?" He dug inside, pulling out the baby jacket we'd bought along with a few clothes Denise had gotten what felt like forever ago.

"Yeah, thank you." I took it from him and walked to the bathroom, not closing the door fully so I could hear Ulric. Luckily Levi went back to him when I was at the bathroom, which made me feel better. Yes. I was now afraid to take my eyes off of him.

"Oh...man" I laughed at my own reflection. I looked a mess...I had a good excuse but still. Taking a brush, I combed out my hair before pulling it back into a ponytail. Then washed my face, brushed my teeth and used the bathroom.

When I finished in the bathroom, I caught Levi just staring at Ulric, gently rubbing his head.

I walked over to him, and asked, "You aren't mad about adding Oidhche, are you? I got a little too excited—and pushy."

He wrapped his arms around me, holding me close, allowing me to rest my cheek on his chest.

"It's perfect, don't worry. Besides, he has my last name … unlike some people."

"Here we go." I giggled.

"You aren't getting out of marrying me anymore."

"I wasn't trying to—"

He put his finger to my lips, and I glared at him. "No more waiting … it's happening this spring."

"Fine."

He eyed me carefully, so I lifted my hand like a boy scout … or something. "Wedding in the spring, for sure. I swear."

Wrapping his arm around me tighter, I rested against him again, holding him just as tightly.

"You know, with a name like Ulric Pierre-Oidhche Black, he's going to be end up a rock star or something?"

"We're *never* going to be cool again, are we?" I asked, and he just nodded, making the both of us laugh.

He kissed the top of my head. "I'll be right back."

Nodding I let go reluctantly as he headed towards the bathroom. Leaving me to smile over Ulric, I murmured softly, placing my finger under his hand. It took only a second for him to grip on.

"I hope you like baseball," I whispered down at him. "If not, just bear with it until we can break it to your father."

"Excuse me."

I glanced up as the new night nurse came in, her old wrinkled arms cradling Ulric's chart. Quietly, she walked over. "Good evening, how are you? I'm Kelly-Ann. How are you feeling?

I grinned. "Giddy."

"As you should be," she replied taking out a baby thermometer and placing it on his forehead.

Being the person I was, I leaned over basically hovering over her shoulder to see.

"Perfect." She nodded, and I relaxed. "With the weather like this, make sure to check his temperature every so often."

"Is everything okay?"

I turned to Levi as he came out of the bathroom, I could tell he'd taken time to wash his face and fix his crazy bed hair. I would have teased him if his green eyes weren't filled with worried as he looked directly at Ulric.

"He's perfect," I repeated the nurse's words and he relaxed, coming over to me. I added, "she was just saying that we need to pay attention to his temperature, seeing as he's a Blizzard Baby now."

"Ahh," he whispered, placing his hand on Ulric's head.

When I looked back to the nurse, she briefly gave Levi a strange look, before she spoke again.

Levi glanced at me, but didn't say anything. We both knew that look. The 'oh...he's the father' look but we were just too happy to care.

PREGNANCY: MONTH 4

LEVI

She barged into my office, arms folded under her now-bigger breasts, and on top of her small, but now noticeable, bump. Her dark brown hair curled into a wave stopping right beside her breasts…which were far too distracting for their own good. She was stunning. Pissed. But stunning.

"We'll talk about this whenever you aren't about to die," Tristan muttered under his breath, rising from the chair on the opposite side of my desk. He quickly gathered up the case files in front of him, and nodded to Thea as he left. "You're glowing today, Thea."

"Thank you, but don't compliment me right now. I want to stay angry," she said, never looking away from me, her brown eyes ready to fire daggers.

Tristan gave me the sign of the cross behind her back, and if she weren't there, I would have flipped him off.

"Thea—"

"Did you give me the Gibbs case because I'm now a human incubator?" she snapped, before I could even get a word out.

I rose from my chair, trying to save myself. "I took the case before I realized you were—"

"A human incubator," she repeated. "That doesn't explain why I'm now first chair. But it does say my fiancé is an asshole."

"Hey!"

"What else do you call a man who makes his pregnant fiancée defend a woman who killed her infant?"

"Accidentally!"

"Don't-fucking-carally!"

"Thea, when I took the case, you felt so bad for her!" I reminded her.

"I didn't know I was pregnant then; it's different now! She makes me so angry! Every time I see her mug shot, I want rip it up into little tiny bits, throw into the trash and kick it out of the window," she said quickly, her hands ripping up imaginary paper, that it took me a second to catch up.

"Come here," I said, leaning on the edge of my desk.

"No. You're going to try to calm me down—"

"Which would be good for both you and our baby." I looked at her stomach. She sighed deeply, walking over to me, and when she was close enough, I put one hand on her side and one hand on the curve of her stomach.

"We find out the sex tomorrow right?" I asked rubbing softly.

"Yes." She sighed relaxing, though she didn't want to.

I grinned, and kissed her stomach, before looking back up at her. "We're never going to make a mistake as bad Rita Gibbs, but we aren't going to be perfect either. Believe me, I Googled how to be a perfect parent but apparently the parenting world is very divisive."

"I know…and mean." She made a face, pouting. "Moms are scary. I just strolled into this clothing store because I saw this cute little take-me-home outfit, and the lady in there went on and on about how mothers who use certain fabrics are monsters … *fabrics*, Levi."

"What fabrics?" Were we supposed to only use—

"Levi." She laughed, shaking her head at me. Taking a deep breath. "I can see she feels bad, and I know you put me on this case because it was a sure victory, having the pregnant woman defend the baby killer…"

"Accidentally killed … and I put you on the case with Raymond because you are a good lawyer," I reminded her but she just went on.

"I feel like I'm going to break down and cry in court. I just got out of law school. The first impression I'm going to make in court is of a sobbing, hormonal—"

"Human incubator," I finished the last part for her. "And so what? I didn't just hire you because I'm screwing you— Ouch! Kidding!"

She glared at me. "Kidding about the joke, or about not just hiring me because you *were* screwing me?"

"First, why past tense? Second, don't try to cross examine me, Mrs. Black; I'm one hell of a lawyer. Third, what do you want for lunch?"

"First, past because I'm slightly annoyed with you and plan on withholding sex. Second, I'm not your wife yet. Third, you keep saying you're one heck of a lawyer, and yet, I just see you in here, kicking your feet up. Fourth, I'm going to eat lunch with my client." She broke out of my arms.

"Future mean-mom-in-training."

"Miss tonight's baby class and you'll see present mean," she said, pointing her finger at me before pulling open the door.

"Love you," I told her.

She smiled. "Love you, too."

"Now, go win my case."

Her smile dropped as she stomped out. Smirking, I picked up the baseball from my desk, and walked over to see the view outside my corner office. Boston—each day it got more and more beautiful. Tossing the ball up and down, I wasn't interested in the skyscrapers but the trees of in the distance. I wanted to move, from our townhouse to something…more. The brownstones were nice but the yards were small, I wanted a yard. Which meant we'd have to go further out of the city, and a wealthy gated neighborhood would be rejected Thea moment she saw it.

"Mr. Black, your missed calls."

Turning, I saw good ol' Betty, glasses hanging off her neck by old beads, her gray hair now cropped short. "Yes, Betty, come in."

She put her glasses back on and looked up from her planner as I moved to my seat, putting the baseball back on the desk. "Judge Holland called and asked to meet tonight for dinner."

"Call him back and tell him I can do a late lunch," I replied, pulling out the logs to sign.

"Okay, and Mrs. Yu wants—"

"Tell her we're working on it as fast as we can, but her son did drive into a hospital building, so it isn't as simple as posting bail."

"And Mr. Thornton?"

"Bloody Thornton." I groaned rolling my eyes. "Tell him…anything. I don't care, we aren't hiring him."

"Lastly, the Gimps."

The Gimps.

The Gimps?

"Who the heck are the Gimps?" I looked up at her.

Her planner was down and she just gave me that old look of hers.

"Betty?"

"If one of those tech boys come to my desk and starts pulling and uploading and software, I'm thinking I'm going to get a hammer and make them gimps. I have system. It might not work as fast or as shinny as their little touch pads, but I like my system. Do you not like my system?"

"Me?" I shook my head, raising my hands in defense. "You're fine."

"Then tell them to stop touching my desk!"

"Yes, ma'am." I nodded to her.

She took a deep breath and took off her glasses. "Good. I'll go make the calls."

"Thank you, Betty," I said in the sweetest tone I could muster as she headed back to her desk.

Grinning, I'd just put my pen to paper when Tristan busted in.

"Does no one knock anymore?" I asked him baffled at the revolving door my office had become.

"Did Judge Holland ask to meet for dinner?" he said abruptly, his brown eyes wide.

I nodded but didn't speak.

"Judge Sotto just retired," he said, allowing me to fill in the blanks.

"…which means there is now a spot open on the circuit," I whispered. "They're looking for a new judge."

"They're looking for you, Levi."

Betty knocked, thank god someone did, before sticking her head inside. "Judge Holland said he can only do dinner?"

"He'll do it," Tristan said for me.

"I can't."

"Why not?"

"Baby classes."

"Feed them when they're hungry. Change them when they need to be changed. Don't drop them. Make sure they are dry and warm. Done."

This time I really did flip him off. "Thank you, Obi-Wan Kenobi."

"Fuck you—"

"Boys."

"Sorry, Betty," we both said.

"So what do I tell Judge Holland's secretary?" She asked.

Good question.

"I'll call Bethan. I'm sure she'll cover for you just this once," he said to me.

"You people are trying to get me killed," I muttered, pulling out my phone to call Thea.

"Think of it this way, you get more time off as judge too." He took the baseball and sat in the chair "And my name gets to be on the wall all by itself. Knox and Associates."

"So that's what you're really gunning for—my seat." I replied disconnecting the phone when she didn't answer. She was most likely with a client.

"Actually, your whole damn office." He nodded behind me. "You have the best view."

"I do, don't I?"

"*The Impeccable Life of Levi Black.*"

I never wanted that movie to end.

THEA

When he came in, I was sitting on the couch, eating vanilla ice cream out of the tub. "Welcome back," I said, taking a bite.

He put his suit jacket on the arm of the chair closest to the television, and pulled off his striped tie before sitting down on the edge. "I'm sorry we missed today."

"I didn't miss anything. I went." I licked the spoon.

"I thought—"

"Bellamy had a fever. So Bethan couldn't go, and she was going to call your mom, but in all honesty, I didn't want anyone else to go with me but you. So I told her I wasn't going, and then went on my own." I wished I hadn't, but I did.

"Thea, I'm so sorry—"

"Stop saying sorry!" I didn't want to yell but ... but I was so upset and seeing him feel bad didn't make it any better.

"Baby?" He moved to sit next to me as I started cry. "Are you okay?"

"I'm crying over ice cream ... does this look okay to you?" I snapped, shoving my spoon in like shovel, lifting it, and stuffing it into my mouth. "I was a strong, independent person before you!"

"I know."

"Then why am I crying!"

"I should have been there—"

"Not just that." I wiped my tears on my arm. "I'm mad about that, but not just that."

"What happened?" He put his palm on my cheek.

Staring up at him, seeing him so worried, made me not want to say it anymore. But he pushed.

"Love, what happened today? Was it Gibbs?"

I sighed, shaking my head. "Do you know what sucks the most about being black?"

He didn't answer, and I knew he wouldn't until I finished my rant.

"Not knowing if some people are just judgmental assholes, or if they are *racist*, judgmental assholes. And I can't say anything until I know, because I don't want to be the girl who cried racism. But you should have seen the lady in charge. She kept picking at me during the class, throwing out unwanted statistics for unwed mothers and minorities, which is code for black mothers. I wanted to tell her to shove it, but everyone was just staring, and I didn't want to leave because … because we paid for the damn class!"

"What's the number of the place?" he asked angrily, reaching for his phone.

"Levi, don't—"

"Fuck that!" he snapped. "I'm going to—"

"It's your fault, too!" I hollered at him, and he froze. "You should have been there like you promised, but you weren't. I don't need you to be my knight in shining armor. I don't need you to save me from people like that, because you can't. They exist everywhere. I need you to be there when you say you are going to be there and stand next to me so I can ignore them … prove them wrong." Putting my ice cream down, I felt around my stomach.

"Are you all right?" He rushed over to me again.

"Yeah…" I whispered, looking down. "I think he's moving."

"Seriously?" He grinned and reached up to touch where my hand had been.

"Can you feel him?"

Frowning, he shook his head.

"I swear, even if the president calls, I won't miss anything else," he whispered, kissing the side of my head.

"Are you becoming a judge?"

He shook his head. "I like having Betty as my secretary, and Tristan as my partner at the firm. But most of all, I love working with you. I'm way too selfish to give all that up."

I smiled, lifting my ice cream again. "Tomorrow, I get to kick ass in court and find out we're having a girl."

"Boy."

"Girl."

He grinned, speaking down to my stomach, "I already have your baseball gloves."

"You're going to have find a girl's size, right, Willow?" I said, looking down at my stomach too.

"Willow?"

"After my grandmother. I'd promised her when I was nine that I'd name my kids after her and grandpa. And now that she's … she's gone … I feel like I should honor that. And before you say anything, remember they get your last name."

"You left me no room to argue." He snickered softly, rubbing my stomach again. "But it's going to be a boy, so what was your grandfather's name?"

"Ulric."

"Ulric," he repeated slowly. "Levi, Thea, and Ulric."

"Levi, Thea, and Willow. It's perfect, right?" I smiled up at him.

"It would be perfect if we all had the same last name, *Ms. Cunning.* But no, Mommy wants to wait."

"Excuse me for not wanting to waddle down the aisle, with no champagne, no dancing, and in a tent of a dress. On top of not be being able to wear my rings because my fingers are huge…"

"Yeah. Yeah. Yeah." He took the ice cream from me. "Sure."

I smacked his shoulder, but he just kept laughing and eating.

"Don't finish it!'

"We have like nine of these."

"I'm eating that one." I snatched it back, and he leaned over and kissed me, his tongue licking the ice cream off mine.

"Ulric, is she even sharing it with you in there?" he asked licking the leftover ice cream off of his lips .

"Don't you see this stomach growing?" I teased, sticking my stomach out more and he leaned over and kissed my lips, licking the ice cream off my mine.

Just as I leaned into him, he pulled back "I have an idea."

"What?"

He got off of the couch and rushed past me, toward our bedroom. Lifting the spoon full of ice cream to my mouth, I shook my head and focused on the TV. I didn't even want to know…

Wait? I should have been more upset with him, shouldn't I?

Why did I let him off the hook so easily…?

"Oh." I glanced down at my stomach as the baby moved around again. "You're on his side already, huh?"

LEVI

"Levi, what are you doing?" she asked as I led her in, blindfolded.

Once she was in, I removed my tie from her eyes. She blinked a few times as her eyes adjusted, and then looked around at all the candles that covered our bathroom, before finally landing on the warm bath drawn for her.

"This is what I wanted, but didn't know I wanted," she said happily, turning back to me.

"Forgive me for missing class then?"

She glared, and I pouted, making her fight the urge to laugh. "Only if you help me undress."

"I'll do one better," I said, undressing her, before lifting her.

"Levi, I'm heavy!"

"Not yet, but getting there." Her hands balled into fists, but the moment her feet touched the water, she forgot all her annoyance and relaxed. Stripping down too, I sat behind her, shivering at the water temperature, it wasn't cold but it wasn't nearly as hot as I wished it to be.

"This is nice." She wiggled a little, getting comfortable, before leaning back against my chest.

Closing my eyes, I listened as she hummed softly, stopping only to ask, "Do you think Kangnam BBQ house will deliver?"

I knew the answer to this question … which meant I was done relaxing for the night.

"I'll order for pick up."

BABY: DAY 7

THEA

"Welcome home, Ulric," I said to him as he stared up at me, with those beautiful hazel-green eyes. Whenever I talked, he always reached up to touch my face. I pulled off the tiny blue and green mitten his grandmother had given him and kissed his fingers.

"*Jesus Christ*, this snow!" Levi groaned as he shut the front door, the car seat in one hand, and our bags in the other, snow falling from his wool jacket.

"It's snowing again?" I asked, turning back. We'd spent the week in the hospital because of the blizzard, which was great because we got a lot of tips and help from the nurses. But on the other hand, we'd been stir crazy and so ready to get home.

"Yeah. Just started again. Looks like it's not over after all," he replied putting our stuff down by the door and taking off his jacket and scarf. He'd gone in out twice, first to help me bring Ulric inside and then again to get our things.

"Hello, Marshmallow," he said, kissing Ulric's forehead.

"Oh no. Don't call him that, or Bellamy will never let it go." I laughed, rocking Ulric, as his little arms waved about.

"Like mother, like daughter," he said, reaching to take off my hat. I maneuvered my neck so he could take off my scarf. "Okay, my turn."

He reached for Ulric.

Pouting, I kissed Ulric's hands once more, before gently settling him into Levi's arms.

"Come to Daddy," he cooed, bouncing him just like the nurses did. Ulric smiled. "Yes, that's right. I'm your daddy. You want to see your room?"

"I'm telling you, all this baseball stuff, and he'll want to take up interpretive dance or something." The moment I said it, Levi looked up at me as if I'd lost my mind, hugging Ulric to his chest.

"Let's go see your room before your mommy tries to ruthlessly crush my heart again," he whispered, headed for the stairs.

Rolling my eyes, I took off my coat, putting it on top of his, as he waited for me.

"I'll get it," he said when I reached for the baby bag and car seat.

"Then you'll have to leave us again. I've got to go." I smiled right behind them. He'd done everything. I knew I gave birth, I knew this was what it was like being parents but still, he was carrying him so why not.

He made a face but Ulric knew just how to make us smile and the moment he looked back down at him, he didn't even worry about it. He walked back up the wooden steps slowly until he got to the top floor. Up next to him, I closed the baby gate and followed him down towards his bedroom.

"What do you think?" he asked, lifting him a little so he could see the room.

Almost all of the walls were a navy blue with the exception of the wall adjacent to Ulric's crib. There, the wall had been perfectly wallpapered with the image of a giant baseball. So it was mostly white with the red stitching of the baseball on the corner. In the center, written in Boston Red sox font, was the letter U...and that was just the beginning. The changing table sat on top of the dresser, which he'd painted red. Written in bold white lettering, it read, "Fenway Park," along with "Red Sox Nation," and the words "World Series Champs," and around that in small numbering the years, "2004, 2007, 2013," and then "20 " with space next to it. Apparently for the year Ulric would win one. Still not done...closing the door, he showed him the jersey onesies he'd gotten in both red and white. The name BLACK embroidered on the back over the number 23rd which was originally my due date.

"What do you think? A champ room for a future champ?" he asked Ulric.

Sitting down on the rocking chair, I watched as they walked around the room, Levi giving him the grand tour. When I met him, he seemed more into music and law than baseball. His house was orderly and elegant. Sure, he had a few baseball things. Like a beer opener and a jersey. But it was Boston, so it was hard to find anyone who didn't have stuff like that. It was only when I moved in, and baseball season started, that he came out like a drag queen at Mardi Gras.

"Pitcher or catcher?" he asked, lifting the baseball mitt in front of him.

Dear God, please let this kid love baseball.

PREGNANCY: MONTH 6

THEA

"I can't believe you're letting them do this." Bethan shook her head. Levi and Tristan were currently painting the nursery, both of them wearing old ripped jeans and crew cut t-shirts, listening to the game on a radio, which sat in the corner on top of the painting surface shields.

"Let them paint, or make the nursery a baby baseball cave?" I asked, cutting lemons for the lemonade.

"Both," she replied, shaking her head as she reached for one of the chocolate cookies. "Tristan tried ... even after we found out we were having a girl, but I told him he could pick three things; he chose a pink baseball bat she doesn't use, a Red Sox shirt I can't find, and a baseball, which she drew on and tried to make a doll out of. Successfully killing his dreams of coaching the next Dot Richardson."

"I have no idea who that is?" But then again I didn't know shit about baseball so what else was new.

"Kickass woman who dominated in the '70s." She lifted her fist proudly, which was weird for many reasons, but the

43

fact she also didn't like softball was the most important. Understanding the look I was giving, her she grabbed for a sugar cookie this time. "Just because I didn't like baseball, doesn't mean I can't proudly applaud anyone who's a kickass bitch in their field."

I smiled. She had a point.

"Excuse me? Ma'am?"

We both turned to see a short, balding, construction worker, standing at the French doors. Bethan looked at me to remind me I was the ma'am he was talking to...because I was...duh.

"Yes? Is everything okay?"

He nodded and handed me a slip. "This is the invoice for the other supplies."

Wiping my hands, I took it, and Bethan leaned in, nosily trying to read it too.

"Fourteen grand for glass? Glass what?!" I gasped, but before he could reply, the paper was snatched away by Levi, who was now wearing a red sox baseball cap backwards on his head. He nodded as he read over it. Then pulled out a blank check from his back pocket. He patted his pockets for a pen and Tristan handed him one while taking one of the cookies.

"Here you go; use whatever is leftover for the ... other stuff," he said, handing him a check and leaving me to watch fourteen grand walk out a pair of white French doors to the unknown.

"What are you building out there? That costs fourteen grand?" I asked him.

"It's more than that, but didn't someone say we aren't joining bank accounts until a time, which you have not yet given." He winked and took one of the cookies. When he did, paused chewing slowly.

"What? Is it bad?" I asked.

"Thea these are—"

"Just practice ones." Levi cut Tristan off taking a couple cookies while Tristan stole juice boxes. Levi kissed my cheek; "Keep at it, we'll get rid of these for you."

"Hey!" I hollered as they made a run for it, laughing. "At least take napkins or something!"

"Children in a grown men bodies." Bethan shook her head as she ate a cookie and I crossed my arms. "What?"

"These are for your daughter!"

She frowned. "Kids get everything."

I laughed at her. Everyone in our families were kids apparently. I moved to get a new tray and more batter.

"How much you want to bet he's making an indoor baseball field out there?" Bethan asked after the boys left the room.

I groaned. I doubted that was the case, but I was tired of baseball. "Why do they love baseball so much? Other than the obvious."

"They played in college, didn't you know?"

I frowned because I didn't, and Levi and I had talked about college a lot. "Only for the first season; they both got in some fight. Levi hurt his shoulder. Tristan was bruised up, but nothing that bad. He felt guilty, though, since he was the one driving."

Putting down the knife, I just stared at her, shocked. "Why has no one told me about this?"

"I think they're sworn to secrecy or something."

"What?"

"I'm serious. I didn't find out for a while after it happened either. And when I'd asked Levi about it, he'd said not to worry. Tristan had just said it was his fault, and Levi had forgiven him. Pretty much it. Guys are weird like that.

I tried to think of what they could have possibly fought over, but nothing came to mind. This would bug me. And not only because I didn't know all the details, but because Levi had never thought to tell me in the first place.

"These are for Bellamy, remember?" I said, as she grabbed another cookie from the plate. "You're crazy ... you know that. If you eat all of this, how will you face those women tomorrow?"

She froze, slowly putting juice back down on the kitchen counter. "I hate them so much. I know I'm not supposed to say that. But Thea ... I. Hate. Them."

"Come on, they can't—"

"They are worse," she said seriously. "Because they are much better at being underhanded than they were as teenagers. I grew up with these people. You know how some families have a black sheep? Well, I was the black sheep of my whole preppy high school. I didn't care about all the stuff they did, and for some reason, that made me the weird one. Whatever. I survived. But now, it's like every time I buy store-bought cookies, I'm a bad mom. I don't spend an extra hour curling my daughter's hair, I'm a bad mom. Which hurts to hear. But what hurts more is that she's now a reflection of me. She's the black sheep's daughter, and I don't want her to just survive. I want her to have a good time and thrive in school."

She put her hands on her head, and I handed her another cookie, which made her laugh and sniffle. "Sorry, I didn't mean—"

"No, it's okay." I'm glad she felt comfortable enough to tell me why she seemed so down. "Truth be told, this whole becoming a mother thing..."

"Is scary," she finished.

I nodded. "Levi and I were talking about it when I worked the Rita Gibbs case."

"The lady who killed her kid—"

"Accidentally," I cut in, and I wished I didn't, because I felt like Levi now.

"You won, right?"

I frowned. "No one won. I mean, she doesn't go to prison, but she still lost her kid. On top of all the other stuff that has happened to her. I mean, she was twenty. Her parents kicked her out for running off with the bastard that eventually left her. She had no money and could barely produce any milk, how was she supposed to know she shouldn't give her infant water sometimes? I didn't know water was deadly to infants did you?"

She shook her head no. "I barely knew how my vagina worked when I was twenty, let alone anything about kids."

"Exactly." Which was why her case, though I won, still made me teary eyed. "She wanted her kid. She loved her kid. It was accident and it was…it was just sad. When you're a mother, one wrong can equal disaster."

"And everyone is judgy. I saw all the girls at Bellamy's school wearing this cute petticoat that came in all different colors. So, I went to buy it for her, and it cost over a grand. A *thousand dollars* for a four-year-old's jacket. I knew it was ridiculous. I knew she'd outgrow it and I'd be throwing away that money, but I felt so bad, I gave in and bought it. And guess what?"

"It didn't fit?"

She shook her head. "The girls started to wear a new coat. I was so pissed. I'm sure one of their moms did it on purpose."

"You really don't want to move another school?" The pressure was ridiculous.

She exhaled deeply. "My mom is on the board of Paramount Hills; Levi and I went there, and it's a good school. Plus, we do get a huge legacy discount, so it's much cheaper than sending her to another private school. One time I joked about sending her to public school and Tristan was pissed saying why do I work so hard if my daughter can't go to the best school blah blah blah."

I laughed at her. If you met both Levi and Bethan you'd never realize they came from such rich families. They were so down to earth and I guess that was because of their parents...well mostly Denise. She'd been a stay-at-home mother. But before that, Levi had told me that since she was a dancer, she'd gotten to meet so many people from diverse backgrounds that she understood how lucky she was. The one story he'd shared was how she had lost a recital to this girl with Mexican heritage. She was obviously disappointed until she saw the girls ballet shoes, which were so old and worn out they were almost falling apart. She'd asked the girl about it and apparently she couldn't afford a new pair, but with the prize money, she finally could. It had left such an impression on her that she made sure to let Levi and Bethan understand how blessed they were.

"Thea?" Bethan asked.

"I was just thinking ... your parents really succeeded with you both." I wiped my hands and waddled around the counter to the gray loveseat, and my back pillow.

"They did, didn't they?" She sighed, and walked to the couch, allowing herself to fall onto it. Turning to me, she smiled softly. "Thank you for baking for me; I really did learn a lot."

"No problem. Just promise, when I'm having a Mommy Freak Out Moment in the future, you'll come to talk me off the ledge."

She laughed. "Deal, but I can tell you'll do great."

"How?"

"You remind me of my mom."

"I'm not sure if that's a good thing, seeing as how I'm screwing her son."

"Ahh…" She groaned, rolling over, covered her face with her hands. "I take it back … don't give me mental pictures."

"Sorry. Sorry."

Calming down, she looked up at the ceiling. "What I meant, is you're kind, and smart, and you can fit in no matter what's going on around you; you make it easy, too. At the last New Year's Eve party, seeing you and Levi, it was like watching my parents again. Totally lovely and regal-like."

"You and Tristan—"

"Are introverts."

"Bethan, you own three bars now."

"Yeah, because…" She thought about it. "I like how everyone just blends into this mess of people. No one is really standing out. Just everyone trying to get drunk and have a good time. Tristan's the quiet and reserved one. I think we have four friends between us."

"Well, until our wedding, you can count me as your second friend," I said to her.

"You are so totally family zoned. Look at you, baking cookies for my daughter, your niece, pregnant with my nephew. Marriage or no marriage, you're family. I'm kinda shocked you guys haven't even set a date yet."

"Shh!" I put my hand on my stomach glanced at the door to the nursery. "Don't get Levi started. He tried to walk me toward the marriage registrar when we were at the courthouse for a case."

"Sounds like my brother." She nodded, drumming her fingers on her stomach. "Is it only the baby holding you back from the wedding or…"

"It honestly is the baby." I wanted to be with Levi. I *was* with Levi. "I never gave much thought about the wedding I wanted … mostly because I never thought I'd find the right guy. And now that I have him, I want everything to be like this storybook."

"Totally like my mom."

"Shut up!" I laughed.

LEVI

Tristan sat beside me, looking around the nursery as he drank one of juice boxes we'd stolen from the kitchen down stairs. "Somebody is definitely going to need to come and redo this shit."

I lifted my phone to show him I was already way ahead of him. I was many things, but apparently not a painter.

"A-for-effort, though," he replied, handing me a juice box. "You going to tell her you're hiring people?"

"Hell no." He had no idea what type of person Thea was. "She'd say it was a waste of money, and then try to do it herself just to prove it. She'd fought me on getting movers, telling me she'd pack herself. A week later, we had only three boxes done, and I'd learned my lesson." Get her to agree, and then get it done as quickly as possible.

"I still can't believe you moved out of the city, so quickly."

"Weston isn't that far." It was thirty-minute drive at most back into the city and while I loved Boston, I didn't want to raise my kid there. I wanted…something closer to what Thea told me about living in Maryland with her grandmother and sister. How she'd roll down the grass in the backyard, or they'd have BBQ and look up at the stars. I wanted the white picket fence.

"How much this place cost again?"

I groaned and looked at him. "Don't ask. Between the main house, and the project out back, my wallet is hemorrhaging."

He laughed. "My father used to tell me the American Dream comes with a hefty price tag, which is why they call it a dream … to make people feel better about not getting it."

"Your father has a talent for making everything depressing."

"Doesn't he? " He chuckled, shaking his head. "I have no idea how his wife has put up this long."

"Third time's the charm."

"Fourth."

"What?"

He held up four fingers. "She's the fourth, and a year younger than Thea."

I stared at him and he nodded.

"How did I miss *that* wedding…?" I paused, thinking. I'd been to the other two with him and Bethan… "You didn't go."

He nodded. "The only wedding I'm going to is yours. After that, I'm done."

"And your daughter's?"

"She's not get married … *ever*," he shot back seriously, and I couldn't help but burst out laughing. "You laugh, but in my mind, she's staying four … forever."

"I wish you no luck."

"Why not?"

"Because if Bellamy stays four, that means Thea stays pregnant … and is that really what you're wishing on me?"

"Fine," he replied, thinking for a second. "Bellamy gets to eight, your kid gets to four, which means he can talk, walk, and at least want to use the toilet by himself. Then we stop this whole aging business."

"Deal." We knocked juice boxes as I leaned back against the one wall we hadn't painted. "What if he doesn't like baseball?"

"Keep having kids. Statistically, one of them must like the sport."

"I knew there was a reason I kept you around."

"You aren't keeping me around, your sister is. You…Well, let's just thank God I've built a tolerance to your ego, oh great and mighty Levi Black."

I cracked my jaw to the side glaring at him, his smug face so proud of his witty comment, apparently forgetting I was both petty and a sore loser. "Maybe it was that tolerance of mine, which made my father think you were *peculiarly strange* and not the right *fit* for Bethan."

He glared back eyeing me carefully. "Bullshit. You're trying to get under my skin."

"Maybe." I shrugged. "Maybe not, ask my father directly…if you can." I grinned sucking on the straw of my juice box.

"You are a *terrible* person."

At that, I laughed. "You knew that and still tried to pick a fight with me."

He opened his mouth, most likely to curse me out, when all of a sudden, he was up and running toward the voice now screaming, "DADDY! DADDY!"

He was out of the room before I stood, and when I got into the hall, my sister pushed me out of the way, rushing toward the spare room. Tristan already had red-faced Bellamy in his arms as she cried hysterically. Thea was at the bottom of the stairs, looking up at me wide-eyed.

"Sweetheart, what is it? What's wrong?" Bethan wiped her face.

Bellamy's lip quivered, and she sniffed. "I didn't know ... where ... I ... I was ... I ... didn't ... see you, Mommy."

Tristan exhaled, relaxing, and kissed the side of her face as she hiccupped. "We came to Levi's house."

"This ... no uncle's house." She pouted, rubbing her eyes.

"Uncle Levi moved to this place now. So we can get ready for Auntie Thea's baby." Bethan brushed her hair. Bellamy reached up to hold on to Tristan's neck.

"We should go," Tristan said to me, and Bethan nodded.

"Bye, princess." I smiled at her when they came closer to me.

She didn't talk, just buried her puffy face into Tristan's chest.

"Once she's like this, there is no talking to her," he explained, placing his hand the back of her head. "We'll come back another time when she's fully awake, and we can finish our conversation."

I'd gotten under his skin.

"Of course." I nodded to him, letting him walk down first, followed by Bethan who carried Bellamy's shoes.

Walking behind them, Thea came back out with a few boxes of cookies.

"Thank you so much, Thea," Bethan said with a hug.

I couldn't look away from them as Tristan put Bellamy into her booster seat, and Bethan went around the other side to sit in the back with her.

"One moment Bethan was falling asleep on the couch," Thea said softly beside me, "and the next, she was up and running for her life. I think I saw her get up before Bellamy screamed. Like her Mommy Senses were tingling or something."

"Tristan too," I said, wrapping my arm around her shoulder. "How do we upload those senses?"

"Let's hope they come when he comes." She wrapped her arms around my waist and squeezed softly.

"Let's hope," I repeated mostly to myself, waving at them as their black Porsche crossover pulled out of the driveway.

BABY: DAY 38

LEVI

"Well!" she hollered, bouncing Ulric in her arms as he screamed his head off, which I didn't know if it was better or worse than the coughing he'd been doing earlier.

"98.9," I said into the phone when I lifted the thermometer off of his head. He started to cough again, his whole face and body bunching up. I hated seeing him like this.

"It's high ... shh."

"At 98.9, he has a slight—"

"Can you not hear him? Doc, this isn't a slight anything!"

"Tell him we're coming to the hospital," Thea said, already reaching for his bag, and I moved to grab their jackets, as the doctor spoke.

"Mr. Black, listen to me. If you bring him all the way here, or to another clinic, he'll scream more, and the air is already cold and dry. Trust me for a moment."

I'd never realized how hard trust was when it came to a child.

"What should I do? What?" I asked, desperately rubbing my forehead.

"Take him to the bathroom, strip him down, and turn on the shower. He doesn't need to get wet ... just make sure there is enough steam. You understand?"

"What is he saying?"

"For how long?"

"After a few minutes, he should calm down. I'll stay on the phone with you."

"LEVI!"

"I'M COMING!" I hollered at her, and I wished I hadn't.

"I know it's difficult, but you need to keep calm."

Trying to acquit a woman of manslaughter when you knew she did it, that was hard ... this ... this was a special level of hell.

"Hold on," I said getting my speakers and turned to the both of them. "He said he needs steam. Take his clothes off in our room, so the shower gets hotter faster."

She rushed out the door and I followed behind, connecting my phone to speaker. "Dr. Cohen, you still there? Can you hear me?"

"Yes, perfectly."

"I'm turning on the shower," I said putting my phone and the speaker down in the middle of the dual sinks as Thea tried to take off his pants and onesie as he kicked her hands, twisting as he cried again.

"Make sure there are no doors or windows open, you're basically creating a sauna."

"Okay," I said though I doubt I heard me as I opened the shower door. I felt so weak...too weak to even talk. I made sure to close the bathroom door and put a towel at the bottom before taking off my shirt and jeans. I sat at the foot of the shower door, the water bouncing off the wall where I angled the shower head.

"Give him to me." I held out my arms.

She came over, gently putting him in my arms and then took a seat right beside us and held his hand.

"He's still crying!" I called out, rocking him gently in my arms.

"Give him a minute."

A minute felt like days. But finally, when it came, he took deep breaths, his chest rising. He even wiggled a little in my arms. But by the third minute, he'd settled down much more, putting his fist to his month.

"Thank God." Thea exhaled, her head on my shoulder.

I swallowed the lump in my throat. *Yeah, thank God.*

"Like I thought," Dr. Cohen voice came through the speaker, startling Ulric, who didn't understand where the new loud voice was coming from. Which was good, he'd been crying so loud he couldn't hear anything else. Thea got up and lowered the volume just a little bit. "He's caught a small cold, which caused him to get a dry throat. Do you have a humidifier?" Dr. Cohen asked.

"No," Thea replied.

"Since you don't already have one, get a warm mist pediatric humidifier. For now, until his next check-up, always have it on around him. This weather hasn't been helping, and while I'm sure the heat is on, that's still just stagnant air."

"How long should we stay in here?" I asked.

"Maybe another three or four minutes. Check his temperature again in a half hour; if it's normal, then that's all it is. If it's climbing, then come in, and call me if you need anything. But from the sound of it, he's feeling much better."

Ulric was now babbling, trying to put his fist in his mouth.

"Thank you so much." Thea exhaled deeply. "Thank you."

"That's why I'm here. Try not to panic too much, all right?"

Easy for him to say. She said goodbye for the both of us and then just sunk to the floor. She put her hand over her mouth and her brown eyes were fighting back tears again.

"Come here," I said to her. "Look at him."

Again, she took another breath before crawling over to him. When he saw her face, he giggled, lifting his hands toward her.

"Apparently my arms aren't as nice as Mommy's," I said.

She stroked his face gently. "I thought..."

"I know." I kissed the side of her head. She had thought the worst ... just as I did. It really felt and looked like he was dying.

"Buy the humidifier."

I turned off the water before walking over to my phone. "I'm going to see if there are any I can pick up tonight."

"He said it was a warm mist pediatric humidifier," she repeated even though I remembered. It was seared in to my brain the moment he said it.

"Shit," I muttered scrolling through each sight.

"All of them are sold out."

"Levi—"

"Don't worry." I said already I dialing the only person on Earth who I knew could get me anything when I needed it.

"Sweetheart?"

"Mom, do you know where we can get a warm mist pediatric humidifier as quickly as possible?"

THEA

"Thea, you look amazing!" Denise said, hugging me quickly to then show me her gift. "I come with a gift."

"I want to kiss you right now," I said, taking the humidifier, which was shaped to look like a toy Panda.

"If anyone deserves a kiss, it's me," Walter shivered as he came into house, his silver hair brushed back and his glasses foggy. "I almost had to trade my liver in for that thing."

"Quite an exaggeration, as if anyone would want your ol' liver," Denise shot back, taking off her scarf, leather gloves, and jacket.

"Old?" Walter said with a glare.

"Thank you, *Mom*, and thank you, *Dad*. I'm glad your *young* liver was not needed," I said to the both of them.

He snickered, giving me one armed hug once he'd taken off his coat. "Where are the boys?"

"Reading," I answered, walking up the stairs.

"Reading?" Denise questioned and I nodded to them as I pressed the code for the baby gate to slide up. Walter being the joker he was looked down as it beeped and closed automatically and said, "Denise look at all these gizmos and gadgets these kids get now, in our day—"

"You were in the office and I was at trying to keep Bethan from taking off her diaper and throwing it in your family heirlooms and Levi was sliding down the stairs on pillows."

Denise: 2

Walter: 0

"You could have at least waited until I finished my statement" he muttered sulking as he walked into the nursery first. "Where is my grandson?"

"Are you all right?" Denise asked, putting her hand on my cheek.

I nodded. "It was scary. But his temperature is down, and his cough is gone. Now that I have this, I feel like I could sing on a hill."

She rubbed my shoulder, and then walked into the room. I followed and saw Walter holding Ulric, green eyes looking into green eyes.

"So you're the one who has me going across the city for a *panda warm mist pediatric humidifier with lights*," he said the last part in a higher voice, which earned him a slap on the back from Denise before she stole Ulric from his arms.

"Panda?" Levi questioned, and I lifted the box for him to see.

"Didn't you say you wanted the panda?" he asked, looking between us.

Levi looked at me, but I shook my head.

"I'm the one who wanted them to have the panda."

Walter's mouth fell open, and his hands went to his hips as he glowered at her. "Tell me you are kidding. I found two other *warm mist pediatric humidifiers*, and you told me no, *twice*, that they had to have the *panda* warm mist pediatric humidifier *with lights*."

"They did, didn't you, Ulric." She cooed at him, and he giggled.

"Why? Why? I had to give up the opening night game seats for a panda?"

"You did what?" Levi frowned, taking the humidifier. "It's nice, Ma, and I'm grateful, but any one of them would have done fine."

"Thank you," Walter replied.

She made a face and looked down at Ulric again. "As your grandmother, I'm telling you to pick any sport but baseball."

"Mom," Levi said with a groan, pointing at me. "I'm already trying fend off her negative mojo."

"Hey!" I smacked his arm, then took the humidifier and walked it over to the table next to Ulric's crib. "Thank you, Mom. I get, and I love it."

"Get what?" Levi and Walter both asked.

I pointed to Levi, and then back to myself. "White. Black. What's both black and white ... the panda and Ulric."

Levi made a O with his mouth as it dawned on him.

But Walter was even more lost. "But pandas are Asian."

He said it so sincerely that I snorted, which one by one made them all laugh. Ulric just looked at us, unsure what was going on, but smiling anyway.

"Have you been getting any sleep?" Denise asked when we calmed down.

"Sleep? What is this magical thing she speaks of?" I looked to Levi.

"Don't remember it well; it's been so long," he played along.

His parents shared a look.

"Go get some rest; we'll watch him tonight, and leave in the morning." Walter stepped up beside Denise.

"Are you sure—"

"Go. It's only a one-night break, and then you must pay your dues like the rest of us," Denise said, and Levi took my hand.

"Thank you, and holler if you need anything," he said, already walking me out the door.

"But..."

"Come on." He lifted me into his arms.

LEVI

"Are you sure it's okay to just leave him with them?" she asked, staring at my parents on the video monitor.

"I'm sure," I said, taking the tablet from her and putting it on my bedside table before lying down beside her. The moment my back met the bed, I sighed happily.

Until she reached over me for the damn tablet again.

"But he could still be—"

Grabbing her wrist to stop her, I looked up at her beautiful brown face. "Love, when was the last time you and I just held each other and slept?"

She stared down for a second longer before laying back down. I pulled her close, so she was resting on me. We stayed like that for barely a second before she popped back up.

"Something is wrong—"

"Thea, he's fine."

"No." She laughed at me before reaching down and taking off her shirt, then her bra. "Take off yours."

She didn't have to ask twice. I took it off quickly.

"Down, boy." She laughed, snuggling against me. "Doctor said not for another week, but I just wanted to feel you."

Disappointed, but understanding, I nodded. It didn't take long before our legs became tangled, and our bodies pressed tightly together. Being this close and unable to have her, but also far too tired to even try was one level above screaming and crying babies in hell.

"Sorry for yelling at you earlier," she whispered.

"When?"

"In the bathroom with Ulric."

Right. I hadn't given it much thought, since we were all yelling. Ulric, included. "Me too."

She reached up, putting her hand on the side of my face, and kissed me. It felt like I was kissing her for the first time all over again. What started off gentle, ended up much more passionate, her mouth opening for my tongue, as I rolled on top her. All her warmness against me, her breasts now too big for my hand, which only turned me on more.

"Levi," she moaned as I kissed her neck. "One more week."

Damn it.

"Ugh," I groaned in frustration, lifting my lips from her skin.

She kissed me quickly, smiled, and said, "One more week, and then your work is cut out for you."

"Why?" I asked, still on top of her.

"I have stretch marks everywhere, Levi." She pouted. "Even on my ass … *my ass*! Not to mention, this little kangaroo pouch, which I'm working on getting rid of. It's going to take your best moves to get me feeling sexy again." She nodded down to her stomach. Was she as small as she was before getting pregnant? No. But I didn't want her freaking out just because she had a tiny belly now. She looked beautiful, and you'd never guess she'd had our child a little over a month ago.

"You are sexy now." I kissed her and pulled back. "Believe me, you're fine."

"Thank you, but I also like my clothes and want to fit into them again." When she said it, I rolled over back on to my slide.

"And here I thought you were worried I wouldn't find you attractive, when all the while you were thinking about your clothes."

She giggled, cuddling up to me more, but I rolled over.

"No, nope, it's fine—"

"Levi." She laid on top of me. "I like clothes, because when I get all dressed up, when you're dressed in your suit, and I walk next to you, I feel like … we're this power couple. Mr. and Mrs. Black. My grandmother always told me the clothes make the person. I know it's lame, but I really love the way people look at us when we walk together at the firm or the courthouse."

Just like that, I was defenseless against her.

"Mr. and Mrs. Black, huh?" I repeated.

She nodded. "March 31st."

"What?"

"Our wedding. I want it on March 31st. I go back to work in April, and when I do, I want to be Mrs. Thea Black, with everything changed—"

I couldn't help myself. I needed to kiss her. Everything that was coming out of her mouth was so sweet. My right arm wrapped around her waist, while my left grabbed a handful of her ass and squeezed.

"One more week, Levi." She said those damn words again.

"Ugh," I groaned out in agony, and she had the nerve to laugh. I slapped her ass and she jumped. "Never laugh at a man with blue balls."

"I'll take my punishment in a week." She smirked seductively.

Closing my eyes, because I couldn't bear to look at her, I said, "Go to sleep, Thea."

"No, *Professor Black*." She whispered and reached under the sheets, taking me in her hand. "I don't want you to be in pain, *Professor*," she whispered innocently. And I didn't dare open my eyes. I couldn't look at her. I'd … I want her too badly.

"Ahh…" My mouth dropped opened as she cupped my balls.

"Yes, Professor, did you say something?"

Clenching my jaw, I took her torture … because there would be a reckoning. I'd get her back for this.

BABY: DAY 39

LEVI

"Good morning, and I'm so sorry! We didn't mean to oversleep," I said, entering the kitchen where my father sat at the island, a bowl of oatmeal, with a side of fruit and glass of orange juice in front of him.

Ulric, in his infant carrier on the counter next to him, was dressed in a new outfit and sleeping soundly. Walking over to him first, I put my hand on his head.

"Don't worry about it. Thea has everything so nicely organized, and he was a sweetheart," my mother said, placing a plate of French toast dusted with powdered sugar, and a side of bacon and egg whites.

"Mom, you didn't have to do this." She used to make this for us on special occasions.

"I wanted to. It felt…" she paused looking at all of us, "nostalgic."

"I'm so sorry!" Thea ran into the kitchen, and my mom put out a plate for her too.

66

"Sweetheart, it's all right. Everyone is fine. Ulric has been fed, bathed, changed, and is sleeping now."

Thea looked to our son beside me, and then back to my mother, wrapping her arms around her.

"Thank you. Thank you for everything."

"We've set a date," I announced before she could say thank you or sorry again.

"Really?" My mother smiled.

And so did I, looking to Thea for her to say it again.

She nodded her head. "March 31st."

"That's so soon!"

"No, it is not," I said quickly, before she made Thea doubt the choice.

"They have a child, live and work together. They are long overdue," my father said with a nod, and I wanted to thank him.

"There is so much to do..." My mother was already reaching for her phone, most likely to call everyone in the state. But then she froze and slowly turned back to Thea. "That is, unless you had other things in mind."

"Anything you want, I want," Thea told her.

"Translation: fork over your wallet," my father whispered to me as I gently rocked Ulric's seat.

"Just when it was recovering from this house," I muttered back.

"It's a good house," my father said, looking around the kitchen.

"Kinda far from work though."

"Not really." The problem with people who lived in cities was the moment anything was more than a few minutes away, it was considered far.

"When do you go back?" he asked.

"It was only supposed to be a month, but after yesterday I'm glad I took off more. I had no idea how in the world Thea would have dealt his coughing and crying alone." Just the *thought* of it was stressful.

"She would have called an in house doctor and after the fourth time, you'd be fighting over why he needs his own personal doctor all the time." My father snickered though he didn't seem to find any of it funny. He looked to my mother again before taking another spoonful of oatmeal. I didn't need to press it more. I could piece it together. It was no secret my father was a workaholic. Some of my earliest memories were of him in his study pacing back forth on the phone, yanking the cord when it got tangled.

I'm glad some of his generations' habits, the whole men must work, were less pushed.

"When does she go back to work? I'm sure she'll want as much time—"

"She wants go back in April."

He looked at me like I was insane. I nodded and he opened his month, but I cut in one more. "I fought for April."

Oh, how I fought and oh how I was thoroughly put in my place.

PREGNANCY: MONTH 8

THEA

"You are acting crazy!"

Grabbing the pillow beside me, I threw it at him. "Don't call me crazy!"

He glared at me, breathing out his nose. "I said *acting* crazy. Acting, because you are not crazy. However, you aren't being logical, Thea."

"Logical?!" I yelled, placing my hand on my watermelon-sized stomach. "Let me remind you of page three, section four, of the Black-Knox and Associates policy and terms—"

"Thea—"

"Employees, upon birth or adoption of an infant, toddler, or young child not yet of grade school age, are entitled to twelve weeks leave, designated by the Employer as FMLA, and shall have full pay during the duration of the twelve weeks which has been given!"

"Section five!" he hollered back. "If the employee wishes to extend FMLA for another four to eight weeks, they may do so, only having given notice to the employer three weeks prior to the completion of their twelve-week leave; however, the employee will do so with partial or no pay at the discretion of the employer!"

"I don't want to extend leave!"

"I do!"

"Then stay home!"

"Thea! Ugh!" He stretched his hands as if he wanted to strangle me, but I simply crossed my arms over my stomach, glaring. "Thea, love," he said softly, sitting on the edge of the bed.

"I'm coming back after twelve weeks; my due date is on the 23rd. That means I start on March 20th, as per *your* policy."

"Exactly, baby, my policy! It's my firm. You are my fiancée, soon to be my wife, and the mother of my child; you do not need to rush back to work. What about Ulric? I don't want him to have a nanny, neither do you, and it isn't fair to drop him off at my parents' everyday while we go work! So what? We bring him to work, too?"

I put my hands on my face, trying stay calm, but I felt like crying. And not understanding he put his hand on my leg.

"I work so hard, baby; what is the point of having money if you can't relax and—"

"You're such a chauvinistic ass sometimes." I tried to ignore the tears as they fell.

He pulled his arm back from its place on my leg. "Excuse me?"

I nodded, repeating, "You're chauvinistic. You aren't saying *we* should take off longer. You're saying *I* should take off longer. Do you really thinking having you as the boss is something I'm happy about? I was your student, but not just any student. I was the daughter of Margaret 'The Shark' Cunning. I had to prove myself to every preppy white kid at

Harvard, why? Because half of them, the ones who knew of my mother, thought I got in because of her. The other half, who didn't know of her, thought I'd gotten in because Affirmative Action. And just when I was proving myself as Thea Cunning, not The Shark's daughter, everyone finds out I'm sleeping with you, and almost overnight I become the Whore of Babylon, sleeping her way to graduation. Every time I came in first, got the highest grade, 'she probably blew him too,' was said. I ignored it. I never talked about it. Because we were happy and in a good place. I graduated at the top of the class, and I ended up working for you. Great, right? I'm no longer the whore. I've proven we aren't just a fling. But now I'm Levi Black's girlfriend, then Levi Black's fiancée, then Levi Black's *baby mama*."

"Who's talking to you like that at the firm?! Why didn't you say anything?" he snapped, leaning forward.

"I told you, I don't need you to play white knight—"

"Goddamn it, Thea!" he snapped, rising up from the bed. "I'm not playing the white knight; I am being your partner! Every time someone insults you or treats you any less than … than anyone else, you don't tell me until weeks … apparently, years later!"

"What am I supposed to do!" I screamed back. "I can't call you to come protect me, I'm a big girl who can—"

"You can, what? Huh? Ignore it? Lift your head up, dig your heels in, and prove them wrong? Meanwhile, you just take the abuse until they come to their senses? You can lie to them. You can pretend as if nothing they say hurts. But I know you, Thea, and I know you're not as tough as you pretend to be! You are not made of stone and neither am I. You can't keep telling me to just stand on the sidelines. You can't keep telling me not to protect you when that is what I am supposed to do! It is what I want to do! Black, white, green, purple, I don't bloody care! If they insult you, they are insulting us. And while I cannot control every racist, bigoted, ignorant asshole in the world, I can and I will control my own goddamn firm!"

I rubbed the side of my head; it felt like my brain was splitting. How could he be both right and wrong at the same time. "Please, sit."

"I'd rather stand," he snapped, still frowning.

"Fine." I lifted the covers, moving my legs over to edge of the bed.

"What are you doing?" He rushed to grab me.

"If we're going to argue, I need to be at eye level with you, and since you won't sit, I'll stand!" *Or, at the very least, fucking try,* I thought, pushing my arm out to brace myself as I tried to stand.

"For the love of God." He sighed, sitting down, and shook his head at me. "Why are you so damn stubborn?"

"Have you ever met a lawyer who wasn't stubborn?"

He frowned, and looked at me, while I tried to speak as calmly as I could, "Levi, you are at the top of the pyramid. Right now, you're about to go defend the governor's wife. I understand, I hear. But hear me. You aren't seeing it from every angle. Shelve our previous conversation, and remember that just because you love me, and I always will love you, that career-wise, we are not on the same level. I'm at the bottom of the pyramid. I'm fresh out of school, and you made me first chair for Rita Gibbs."

"And people thought that was favoritism?" He inhaled, fighting to keep his voice down too. "I knew you'd win and you did. Plus, you being pregnant was—"

"Was part of the strategy of winning. I know." I got him. I got us. But it also didn't help me. "But how did you know I could do it, Levi? You were my professor for a year. Fine. I shadowed you during that time. Fine. Atticus also got to first chair a case. I know. But they aren't seeing me as lawyer. They don't think I've earned it. They think that, once again, I'm using my body or something other than my brain and skill to win. Don't you remember how cutthroat it is fresh out the gate? Everyone is trying to get to the top. To prove themselves, to have name recognition, and respect. To be like you, Levi! Even me. I'm still battling people. You told all the new associates there were four slots for the six of us. They hate me because they know you aren't going to fire me. So I can't earn respect. People are either buttering me up or talking behind my back. If I take off more than twelve weeks, when I go back … Levi, you might as well just make me your secretary. No," I paused, remembered Betty, "you might as well make me Betty's assistant."

His gaze softened, and I'm sure he understood that part at least. He rubbed his forehead, not sure what to say. We sat in awkward silence. Not for long, though, when there was a knock at the door.

"Come in." Levi stood again.

Selene stuck her head in slowly, and then opened the door wider. "It got quieter so I figured everything was good now?"

Levi grabbed his jacket and his files, coming over to me and with a kiss, his hand on my stomach. Selene moved to the side, leaning against the door, when he approached.

"If you need anything—"

"Totally have that covered," she replied, lifting the bag of snacks and smiling at him.

He nodded and looked back at me. "I'll call you before the trial."

"Good luck."

He didn't reply like he usually did, which hurt. He just walked out and Selene stuck her head in, waiting for him to leave. Once he left, she rushed over and jumped onto his side of the bed.

"Pop or Kettle." She lifted the bags for me to see.

"Kettle." I pouted, taking the bag from her and ripping it open. "Was I hard on him? He just wanted me—"

"Exactly ... he wanted," she said, opening her popcorn. "Not what you wanted. And what you want is important."

I looked over to her, really taking in the woman now sitting in front of me. Selene was a rainbow, completely different than how she was a few years ago. Her brown hair had finally grown out into these soft curls. Her curls stopped at her shoulders, kind of like mine did when I let it out naturally. If only had time and half the talent she did for styling. Her fashion had also changed. Gone were the greys, blacks, and burgundies, and now you could always see her coming from a mile away, dressed in bright yellows. Her brown face was always glowing. I nearly cried at the pink dress she'd worn last week.

"What?" she asked, stuffing her face with popcorn.

"You're so beautiful, you know that?" I told her. "I'm really proud of you."

She paused sitting up and crossing her legs. "Thank you. I'm happy you are, but ... remember, I'm your sister, not your kid."

"Of course—"

"I'm not trying to be mean," she said quickly. "And I'm not trying to say anything you said is wrong...I mean...I'm not a kid anymore, Thea, you can count on me. I'm your sister, not your daughter, meaning you can burden me with your problems. If not, I don't want to talk about what's going on with me with you."

"What's going on with you?" I sat up, facing her, and she made face at me. "I'm coming off mom-ish again?"

She nodded, picking up my kettle corn and handing it to me, before continuing to eat hers.

"Fine? How about…" I tried to think of the way Bethan spoke to Levi. "Please tell me your life is much more interesting than mine?"

She smiled. "Better."

Smiling, too, I grabbed the apple juice from her bag. "Well, is it? Any wild frat parties on campus?"

"Trying too hard." She shook her head.

"Fine, Miss Know-It-All! You start the conversation."

"Perfect." She laughed, winking at me. "And, yes, there are parties, but they aren't frat parties. More like football parties, and I'm usually good at parties, but this last time … I felt like odd man out."

"Why?" I asked, before stuffing my mouth.

"Funny enough it's kind of the same reason as you." She turned, relaxing against the pillows.

I laughed. "DeShawn is the boss at the firm where you're working? And everyone but him and his best friend, who is also the boss, is ready to trip you down stairs when you're around? And are probably glad you're stuck on bedrest while they all battle to be on the governor's wife's case."

"No…" She stared at me.

"So not the same … but go on." I stuffed my mouth.

"First of all, the governor's wife probably doesn't like being referred to by her husband either."

"Huh!" I scuffed, lifting my head. "I call her the governor's wife, because watch her whenever she's on camera; she comes on and says, 'Hi everyone, I'm Governor Eilish's wife, Dorothy-Ann Eilish... every single time. Some women want be ornaments on their husband's tree. While I was at Harvard, I overheard some of the undergrad girls talking about how they only went there to find a smart guy to marry. They wanted to spend the rest of their lives at home. And I'm not knocking stay-at-home moms, believe me, but they were spending thousands of dollars, per year, in order to find a tree to hang themselves on. I wanted to tell them eHarmony was much cheaper! They had no goals, no dreams, nothing but getting married so that someone could take care of them. It was scary. I didn't think women like that existed. But they do. Dorothy-Ann most likely felt her husband was spending too much time with his intern, and she didn't want to be the governor's ex-wife, so she killed her."

There was not a doubt in my mind she was guilty, and I wasn't saying it from an outsider's point of view. I'd seen all the reports and watched as Levi built his case. She did it.

"Wow."

I glanced over to her, and she was just shaking her head at me. "What?"

"Nothing, just ... I think I saw a dark, twisted version of my future pass before my eyes."

"Huh?"

She finished off the bag, tilting her head back for the crumbs before looking at me again. I just waited, fighting of the urge to bombard her with questions.

"At that party," she said, picking up where she left off. "Everyone was talking about DeShawn. It was like walking with a celebrity. They had just won the game, but DeShawn, he stood out … like always. And when he was talking to guys and I was getting a drink—"

"Of what?"

"Sister. Remember." She smiled.

This was not going to be easy. "You went to get a drink and…?"

"And then a few girls came over, asking what team DeShawn wanted to play on."

"What team?" I questioned, confused.

"Exactly." She pointed at my face. "That is exactly what I said and how my face must have looked. I told them, like a total dumbass, he plays for Georgetown, and he wasn't going anywhere. They laughed and said, 'Duh, we mean in the NFL.' The NFL, Thea, the bloody National Football League. I never thought about it like that. Like, *oh my boyfriend might be in the NFL*. Everyone was talking around me about my future … no, DeShawn's future, with me added into the mix because I was *his girl*."

"Breathe." I rubbed her shoulder, and she fell back on the pillows. "What did DeShawn say? Isn't he majoring in computer science?"

"He's an engineering major, minoring in computer since … the show off." She pouted, and it was cute … and it reminded me of me, too.

"I know. Why couldn't he just be a stupid jock," I teased, but she didn't laugh. "Does he even want to play for the NFL?"

"His exact words were, '*Yeah, that would be cool.*'" She bunched her face and made her voice deeper to mock him. "I had to push to get a direct answer, which was worse. He said he wants to go to the NFL, and he wouldn't work as hard if he didn't. But he also knows that anything could happen and he doesn't want to end up like his father, who got a full ride to Notre Dame, blew out his knee, forcing him quit football, drop out of college and spend the next nineteen years drunkenly talking about what could have been every time he lost a job. Which is why he must take his major seriously, so he has a strong back up. He's thinking about everything. He's laying out two paths for himself."

I could see it. That look in her brown eyes. I knew it well. The doubt. The urge to bolt. But I didn't want her to run, not from him. He was reasonable and trying to make something of his life. He shouldn't be faulted for that. But Selene was my sister and I knew what that doubt was. I knew that fear and how it quickly it squashed the light that was finally shining in her.

"You don't know what you want to do." I spoke out her fears. "You don't want to be his ornament, but you don't know how to be your own tree. And the more he shines, the more his shadow gets thrown on you."

Her brown eyes glazed over with tears she fought back. "I really care about him. I love him a lot, but … I'm not ready to walk down his perfect path—either of them. I've been searching so hard at school to find classes or programs I like. But nothing. Everyone is flying forward, and I'm just the lost bird."

I thought for a second, shifting for the ten thousandth time since no position was comfortable for more than a few minutes.

"Finish the semester, and then take a year off," I whispered.

"Who are you, and where did my sister go?"

Ignoring her, I let all the thoughts come together until I saw the big picture. "In law school, I learned we shouldn't shy away from our connections. We shouldn't soften because of them, but we shouldn't be afraid to use them. Connections were like having a hidden dagger on a battlefield. Just because your enemy didn't have it, didn't mean you had to disarm yourself—"

"Now I remembered what my second point was," she cut in. "Is law school like *The Hunger Games?* It's like they are preparing you for war, not court."

Before I could answer, my phone buzzed, and I had to stretch for it.

Sorry, can't call. We're getting started now. Sorry for not understanding. I'm going to have to stay in the city 'til the trial is over. Do you want to stay at the house, or do you want to come with and stay at Tristan's place?

I glanced at Selene who was staring at me, waiting.

I'm good here. Sister bonding time is needed, I replied.

I'll come back tonight to get some stuff, and I'll check in, so keep your phone close, please. Love you, and I do understand. We'll talk more after this over.

Okay. Love you too. Good luck ... for the second time.

"*Luck only tips the scale if you're good enough without it. I'm more than good enough. ;)*" He finally said. Before I could reply, he sent another text.

"*Starting, don't forget to record! Love you bye.*"

"Did you two kiss and make up?" Selene teased.

"Maybe." I stuck my tongue out at her. "Can you hand me the remote on his bedside table?"

She handed it to me, but looked around the room. "Where is the television?"

I pointed the remote forward, and automatically the mirror blinked once before turning on as the television.

"Well excuse me, then."

"He loves his gadgets," I said to her, flipping to the news. There he was, dressed in his navy suit with the burgundy tie I'd gotten him, but what really turned me on were his glasses.

"You're recording it?" she asked, when the option came up.

"Because it's war." I muted it and turned back to face her. "You asked if they were preparing us for *The Hunger Games* or something? There are two types of lawyers, the ones that truly want to make a difference, the social justice warriors. They are fighting a war against those who are greedy and cruel and oftentimes rich. Then there are those who are lawyers because the love the thrill of it. Yes, we do care about our clients. But honestly, it's a thrill and the war is…it's more complex just like the law. At the first level, it is a battle between minds. Not just with the other lawyer but yourself. Because in order to defend your client you need to know how to prosecute them. The other lawyer shouldn't have something up their sleeve you don't already think about. On the next level, it's not only in your hand. One juror could refuse and the whole jury can be hung. So you have to figure out how to get them on your side. Look." I sat up again leaning in and pointing the television. "See he's wearing his glasses while the prosecutor is opening. He is taking notes, he doesn't need to, but it looks like he is only listening to her as she speaks, giving her his full attention and ignoring the jury."

"But I thought you said you wanted them on your side?"

I grinned nodding as I watched him get up and take off his glasses. "That's what makes him so good. At least one of them already is. When the prosecutor is accusing the defendant, out of habit, we always look to see not only who it is we're talking about but how they react to the accusations at least once…sometimes even more than that. So while he was pretending to listen intently to the prosecutor they are all looking at him. And what they see isn't some cocky sleaze-ball lawyer trying to get a murderer off. They see a handsome, serious, man giving his full attention first, to a woman, second, to the case. See, now he's taken off his glasses to speak to them during his turn. In the back of one of their minds, they'll realize he only uses the glasses when he's reading and writing. Believe me, whatever he's writing is chicken scratch, but to them it looks like he's really doing his homework. So at least one of them will be more inclined to take everything he says more seriously. One of them will weigh each thing he says more importantly because he looks like the bookworm and the facts guy. And that one person is all he needs to hang the jury."

"All of that from him writing, and taking off his glasses?" She laughed at me. "Jeez."

"Exactly." I smiled leaning back again. "That's why he's the best. From the moment he stepped into the court room, he was setting up his battleground." I looked at her again. "I want to go back to work not just because I want to prove myself, but because I love this. I love being a lawyer. I love working to win. And ,yes, I win for bad people sometimes and that sucks, but I can't not love the win. I'll love this baby when he comes. But I'll always want to be a lawyer. That is what it is like to be passionate and that is what I want you to be. So I'm going to use you."

"Huh, how?" She twisted her bottle cap.

"You can lean on me," I reminded her. "If you want, take a year off school, and live here with us, rent and food free, as you search for your passion. In return, you help me take care of Ulric while I'm at work. I don't want you to feel like I'm just dumping my kid on you, so—"

She launched herself into my arms. "Thank you! Oh my God! I've thought about dropping out, or getting a job or something. I was scared I was just chickening out of school, and I didn't want to let you down. But I didn't know what to do."

"It's only for year! And you must keep your grades up 'til—" She kissed my cheek repeatedly.

"You are the best sister on Earth. I swear I'll be the best aunt nanny in the world."

I couldn't help but laugh. I was her connection, because I could afford to take care of her no matter what. I didn't want her to go through the motions in life. I didn't want her to just be stuck. She should be free and passionate about something. If there was anyone in the world I could trust with my child, it was her."

"You do know you have to tell DeShawn, right?"

She froze, and I picked up the remote.

"Good luck with that."

Thank God I was done with the whole dating and trying to find myself thing. That shit sucked.

BABY: DAY 42

LEVI

Watching as she explained every inch of Ulric's room for the third time, I could not help but feel a strange sense of déjà vu.

I'd been in this same exact situation … from a different angle. Instead of standing at the entrance of the door, patiently waiting as I was now, I'd once been in Selene's position. I'd once, not so long ago, held a newborn, Bellamy, staring at her mother, my sister, like she was a crazy person. We were leaving for one night. No, we weren't even leaving! We were going into the backyard, because she'd have a damn panic attack if we had to actually drive anywhere.

It was madness, and yet, if she wasn't the one doing it, I'd be double-checking that there were enough bottles.

"Do you need me to repeat anything?" Thea said, taking a deep breath as she turned to her sister, happily bouncing Ulric and wiping the bubbles he blew. "Selene?"

"Huh?"

Why Selene? Why?

Thea's brown eyes widened, and Selene looked to me.

"I have him. I've downloaded the humidifier app, which, to be honest guys, really? An app."

"He needs it on..."

"On setting three. Use the water bottles with the blue cap to refill it. He's eaten but will leave me with one great surprise in his diaper, and so you've laid out *SIX* new ones for me, along with his wipes, and butt powder...You've brought out four night outfits just in case...I don't know if he's the incredible hulk and rips them when he burps or something. His room is at room temperature in the house app that Levi put on my phone, which will let me know if it gets too warm. The alarm code is the first digit of all of your birthdays, but never fear if I forget there is also an alarm app on my phone too. But the best app of them all is the *sock buddy*. I take this little green sock and put it on his foot when he goes to sleep which make sure his heart rate is fine and he's breathing. I don't have to worry about walking up and down the stairs with him because gasp look there is a mini fridge in my room along with a microwave, so I don't have to go down stairs. Ulric, aren't we lucky huh, mommy and daddy set you up with the hover parents starter pack collection." Selene continued, repeating everything Thea had outlined. In great detail.

Thea frowned, and I came over, putting my hands on her shoulders. "Okay. Okay. We're hovering away now. If you need us—"

"I won't need you," Selene butted in. "Now please, take my sister so she can enjoy what is left of her birthday."

I glanced at my watch. Shit.

"She's right, let's go."

"Love you." She kissed Ulric's cheek.

"What about me?" Selene laughed.

"We'll see after tonight," Thea shot back.

"She loves you. I love you. And I love him. Come on." I kissed the baby's head and took Thea's hand.

"Have fun!"

Oh, I planned too.

"You are far too excited," she said, walking down the steps.

I grinned. "Am I?"

"At least I'll finally get to see this project."

Finally, was right. It had taken much longer than I thought it would. I was surprised her curiosity didn't get the best of her—then again, when did she have time?

"Jackets. Boots. Gloves. Hats. Scarves?" She lifted everything I'd laid out in the living room.

"Having fun?" I asked her.

"It's my birthday. I'm allowed." She kissed me.

"Don't let me stop you then."

Just as I stepped toward the door, Ulric's cry rang out loudly, and she was already turning around to run when I grabbed her arm. "Levi—"

"We aren't here. Your sister has him," I reminded her.

"I know, but maybe I should…" Thankfully, the crying ceased.

"See … after you."

I held the French door open.

"I have no idea where we are going, so lead the way, Mr. Black," she begrudgingly said. Rolling my eyes, I took her hand.

"You're such a dork." The corner of her mouth turned up.

"The dork who gets the girl is no ordinary dork," I reminded her.

"True." She linked her arm through mine as we walked off the patio deck, down the first the steps, and around the pool, on to the grass.

"I can't believe it's getting dark already," she whispered, putting her head on my shoulder. I glanced up at the dark pink-orange sky, mentally crossing off watching the sun set for the night.

"Me either." I said leading her down further.

"Levi?" She frowned when she came off the freshly cut grass of our backyard. "Where are we going?"

"Come on," I said, still walking down the snowy path into the woods. And, as it got darker, as the sun set behind the snow-covered trees, she held on tighter to me. Ready to make a run for it if she needed to… *the big baby.*

"This is by far the creepiest birthday…" Her voice trailed off as she saw the lights. Her mouth fell open, and it was like watching a kid in a candy store.

"You were saying?" I teased, walking toward it.

"Levi," she said in disbelief.

I couldn't help but grin. "I've wanted this since I was a kid and heard it on Floyd Freeman's album—"

"Freedom with a Vengeance, track nineteen, '5 Dollar Town'." She grinned, covering her mouth. "Levi! No way!"

"I was born in a 5 Dollar Town, where everyone's skin was colored brown, and there was no playground. To my right, south-ie, loud and proud. To the east, the police. To the north, where I held no worth, and in the west I needed a vest…"

"Trapped in this box the only place was down or up and so I built my castle up in the treetops." She sang so excited she ran towards me. I caught her tightly and laughed, knowing she was probably one of only maybe one hundred people, myself included, in the state who knew who Floyd Freeman was.

"You built me a tree house."

"So selfish," I whispered, wrapping my arms around her. My lips right beside her ear as I reminded her, "I built us a tree house."

No, this was more than a tree house. It was too luxurious for that. It was made of wood, of course, but had large windows, facing the sun. She broke out of my arms and rushed up the spiral staircase, up the base of the tree, until she got to the deck. I followed. It honestly was much better than I'd expected. It wasn't massive, but it wasn't meant to be; it was meant to be our getaway. The wooden canopy bed the focal point in front of the windows, beside it on the right, a hand carved table for two, with a small fridge in the corner, to the left a standing shower beside the hot tub. Outside was a deck a rope woven hanging bench, and my old guitar resting beside it.

"Like it?" I asked, knowing already that she would.

"Of course. But, you know, a simple birthday dinner at a restaurant would have worked too." She turned back around to face me, and the look in her brown eyes ... that was far more beautiful than anything else in here ... anywhere.

"True." I grinned. "But that would have required clothes."

"Yes." She reached up and pulled off my hat. "The last thing I want between us now is clothes."

I pressed my thumb against her lips, failing horribly to not be eager. "Forgive me."

"For?" She kissed my thumb.

"For not being more gentle," I confessed, leaning to kiss her.

"Who said I wanted gentle?"

The moment the door closed behind us, everything happened far more quickly than I planned. One moment I was on my feet, the next she was pushing me on to the bed. yanking her coat off as well as my own. Her pants and boots came off and she sat right on top of me. Lifting her shirt overhead, I sat up kissing between her breasts as she shoved her hands down my pants. I kissed up her neck as she grinded against me. My hands lifted up her bra, gripping on to her breast.

"Ugh…" We moaned together as her tongue entered my mouth. She allowed me to move my hands between her thighs, and she gasped, breaking away from me.

"Levi." Her lips parted, her hand on my chest. As I held her in the palm of my hand, I could feel her melting.

"You have no idea how badly I've wanted you…" I whispered, taking her nipple between my teeth. How eager I was to fuck her crazily … and make love to her for hours. But a quickie first … just to … just to … ahh fuck…

"Levi … please." She rocked against my fingers; every time she spoke, it was glorious. I was so hard I could barely think straight, yet seeing her like this, I could handle it. I could keep holding off.

But apparently she couldn't.

"Thea." I jumped when she grabbed ahold of me. My head tilted back as she stroked me. She couldn't do this. I was already on the edge, my vision hazy.

Not like this.

I wanted to be in her when I came. Gripping her waist, her brown eyes met mine, as I slowly lowered her onto me. My mouth dropped open, and my whole body shivered at how she sucked me in, her walls tight around me.

"Fuck." She hissed, hands were gripping on my shoulder as I slide in and out of her. Sweat coated all of her, and I licked the drop that rolled down her neck.

"I can't..." she muttered, slamming herself harder against me.

"Jesus," I moaned, holding on to her as I thrust harder, matching her movements, the whole bed rocking with us. Sweat rolled from my forehead into my eyes, and even as it burned, I couldn't stop myself from going deeper and harder into her.

"Levi!" She sang out, but I was nowhere near done and letting myself enjoy how her breasts bounced freely as her nails dung into my arms.

Kissing her, biting her lip, squeezing her ass as she rocked from the force of her orgasm ... I took pleasure in it all.

"Thea!" I gasped, finally spent, and we both collapsed onto the bed. Her breasts against my chest. My hands on her back. The smell of sex that we both breathed in, breathing each other in.

"Both of us were a little eager." She giggled on top of me.

Smirking, I ran my hand down her back. "Eager is good."

"Kinda like the first time we were together?" She rested her head on my chest.

"We need to have sex in our car again," I said, remembering.

"Not comfortable." She kissed my chest and frowned. "Only when we're really desperate."

At that, I smirked. "Deal, until then..."

"Shower."

I fucking loved her.

THEA

His hands gripped my thighs, lifting me up and toward the shower, only putting me back on my feet when we were both inside. Staring into my eyes, he turned on the faucet, and I shivered, my nipples hardening under the coldness as the water rained down on us.

"We can do this one of two ways, Mrs. Black: hot or cold."

"Cold is…"

"Gentle." He kissed me softly, his lips lingering on mine.

"And hot?" I whispered when he broke away.

He smirked, turning me around. I braced my hands on the shower wall as he grabbed my breast from behind and squeezed.

"Take your pick." He bit my ear.

"Hot. Definitely hot."

He let go of one my breasts as he changed the water temp. I shivered as the hot water poured down my back. One of his hands traveled the down my back, and gripped my ass, as the other found its way between my thighs.

"Levi," I gasped, my hand gripping his between my legs.

"Relax, and rock with me, baby," he whispered, and I bit my lip as his fingers went in and out of me quickly.

"Levi … I…" I couldn't even form words; my body was on fire, in all the right ways.

Breathing deeply, he pressed me back against the wall and I could feel him against my back.

"Ah…" I bit down on my lip as he entered me.

SLAM.

"Jesus," I cried out, my eyes rolling back as he fucked me.

"No, just me." He pinched my nipple when I turned to the side he kissed never once stopping as he thrust forward into me.

Our tongues rolled over each other's.

"Fuck," he groaned, when he broke away from me. He grabbed onto both sides of my waist, and all I could do was brace myself against the shower wall. The heat of the water dripping down on us was nothing compared to the heat of him as he...

Slam.

Slam.

Slam.

"Fuck ... I ... yes..." I cried out, barely able to breathe. Trembling at the force of him. I felt myself sliding down to the ground but he held on to me tighter. "Levi..."

"Ugh," he moaned from behind me, kissing my neck.

LEVI

"I'm blaming you," I whispered, leaning back and closing my eyes.

"You can't blame me for anything on my birthday." She laughed. "So, for the record, what are you *not* blaming me for?"

I opened my eyes and stared up at the wooden ceiling; "I had a plan. Show you the treehouse. Open a bottle of champagne. Make love. Listen to some albums. Dance maybe. Then eat. Eat cake. Lick icing off you. Fuck you mad. Then hold onto you until the morning, and give you your Valentine's present. But no ... someone just *had* to jump me."

"Me jump you!" She gasped, turning around to face me.

I nodded. "Yes, jump me. Round one … who was on top?"

Her mouth dropped open, and she tried to move away, to the other side of the hot tub. "Someone couldn't hold himself back, and suddenly it's my fault. I see how it is—wait, Valentine's Day present?"

She sat on my lap and stared me down.

Tiredly, I smirked at her.

"Levi…"

"Shh…" I knew she hated when I did that, but I also hated it when she complained that I was doing so too much. "If anything, you deserved it after the last weeks of pregnancy."

She groaned, laughing at herself as she put her head on my shoulder. "It's weird. I barely remember the pain."

"Oh, I do." I'd never forget.

PREGNANCY: MONTH 9

LEVI

"I want him out," she cried, bouncing as she paced back and forth in the bedroom. "Why isn't he coming out? He was due over a week ago. Make him come out!"

What could I say?

I was so tired, I knew I didn't have anything intelligent to add to this conversation.

"Please come out ... please." She rubbed her stomach, tears streaming down her face. "I'm not sure I can do this. Levi—"

"Shh." I got up off the bed, trying to reach out for her, but she smacked my hand away.

"If you can't get him out, then don't shh me!" I sat back down on the edge of the bed. "We've had sex. I've eaten so much spicy food I could breathe fire. I've tried yoga, I hate yoga, and walking and rubbing my boobs! Even damn castor oil! I've done my time; why won't he come out?! I've been trapped in bed for the last month. I've given up wine, and you know I like wine. I've had to pee every ten minutes. I haven't see my toes in God knows how many weeks. I can't shave anything; I swear I've gotten ingrown hairs. I waddle like a fat duck. I can't sleep comfortably, because now, if I lay still, he kicks the hell out of me. Come on! Please. Please—ahh!"

When she clenched the side of her stomach, I went over to her.

"Are you—"

"No!" she screamed. "He's kicking! He's going to be a handful! He's kicking me for yelling at him! Oh, you better … be so cute or else I'm returning you."

I snickered, helping her onto the bed. "I'm not sure that's how it works."

She glared at me for a moment before putting her hands on her face. "I'm tired, Levi. I'm so tired."

"I know." I kissed the top of her head. "I know, baby, but it's almost over; he can't stay in there forever."

Reaching into my pocket, I pulled out my phone, yawning, but immediately closed my mouth when she glared at me again.

"Are you tired?" she asked softly … a little too sweetly, and I knew it was a trap so I shook my head.

"Me? No. Hello?" I asked, getting up off the bed.

I glanced down at her as she tried to sweetly talk our son into coming out, and answered my mother. "She's … hanging in there."

"Poor thing, just try to remain calm. Rub her feet too—"

"Mom, I got it. Enjoy the New Year's Party, and don't worry about us, okay?"

"It's not the same if you're not here … all of you."

"Next year, all of us will be—"

"Or he could just stay in for another full year. Who knows, maybe I'm a frilled shark." She threw her arms up in frustration.

"A what?" I shouldn't have asked, but apparently, I couldn't help myself.

"Did you know a frilled shark stays pregnant for three and a half years. I didn't, but since I was stuck in bed for a month, I got to learn all about them. For three years, they are stuck swimming about in the ocean, holding up to six kids in them. Meanwhile, the male sharks are just going about their lives. Sleeping in whatever comfortable position they want. Sneaking scotch when they don't think anyone will notice…"

"Mom, I'm going to call you back," I muttered into the phone, only to hear her laugh at me as I hung up.

"Thea…"

"Nope. No. It's fine. I understand you went out on business … cool." She muttered rubbing her stomach.

At this point I was desperate, sitting back on the bed and putting my hand on her stomach. Trying not to smile when I felt him kick because I knew how much it hurt her but I couldn't help it.

"Son," I spoke to her stomach. "For the sake of my sanity, please—"

"Your sanity?"

"Would you like ice cream?" I cut in again; she crossed her arms and didn't say anything.

Nodding, I got back up. "I'll be right back."

"Sprinkles on top!"

She didn't have to remind me. In fact, it was hard to forget because it was all she wanted now. Vanilla ice cream with rainbow sparkles and hot chocolate. I was doing my best to be calm, but she was driving me up the damn wall.

Everything I said bothered her. Everything around her annoyed her. I wanted to bang my head against the wall and beg for this kid to come out alright. And the doctors wouldn't induce for another two days. Two days. Forty-eight hours. I could do this...

"LEVI!"

"I'M COMING!" I hollered back, grabbing the hot chocolate.

"LEVI!—"

"THEA, I SWEAR—"

"THE BABY ... UHHH!"

Everything fell out of my hands as a chill worked its way up my spine. Hearing her cry out again, I ran down the hall and up the stairs three at time before making it into the room, where she at on all fours, the water stain on the bed obvious as she gritted her teeth.

"You swear, what? AH ... UH!" she cried, rocking back and forth. I just stood there. "LEVI!"

"Right! Right!" I said, rushing to grab the baby bag by the door, my keys, and wallet, while trying to think what else we needed. "Do I have everything?"

"No, me! You're forgetting me!" she screamed, and I rushed beside her, helping her walk. "Ahh ow ... it hurts ... ughh!"

"AHHH!" I hissed as she grabbed my arm like she was trying to break it.

"Ohhh." She exhaled, as did I.

"Come on." I ushered her forward slowly, holding her tightly when we got to the steps. Why she'd gone upstairs today of all days was beyond me, but I couldn't tell her that. Slowly, we walked and walked until we made it into the garage.

"AHH! Damn it!" she cried, reaching out to grab me again but I ducked rushing to throw the bag into the back and racing in front of the corner.

"Just breathe, baby. Just breathe—"

"I am breathing! This is me breathing! AHHH." She gritted her teeth, reaching out and grabbing my thigh as I pulled the car out.

Biting my lip as her nails dug into my skin kept me focused on the road, hitting the Bluetooth to dial our doctor.

"Levi, how is everything—"

"He's coming!" Thea hollered into the phone.

I nodded. "We're on our way to the hospital now, Doc—shit!"

"What?" they both said.

Thea simply looked up and out into the traffic, and then repeated after me, "Shit."

"We're getting stuck in traffic—"

"How far apart are the contractions?"

"I don't know … like four or five—"

"Three! Three minutes … ahh … ahh…" Thea started crying, gripping on to the dashboard.

"I want you both to be calm but…"

"Ohhh! AHHH!! I need to push!"

"What?" I yelled at her. "We aren't that far—"

"I need to push!" she cried out.

"Quick, Labor and Delivery," Dr. Cohen stated on the phone. "Levi, pull over on to the shoulder."

"You've got to be—"

"Pull over!" she screamed, already yanking down her sweats.

Doing as they said, I pulled onto the shoulder lane.

"Do you see the head?"

"The head—"

"Yeah ... yes..." Thea laughed and cried and looked up to me, but I could barely see her through my blurred vision.

"Okay, breathe slowly. Levi, support her. Thea, reach down, support him." I grabbed her shoulders, as she cried out.

"Okay, Thea, push with the contractions. As the baby's head begins to emerge, support his head, but do not pull on it. Hold the head in a slightly downward position, okay? Levi, check her hands."

I did, and I saw him. My son, the dark brown wisps of his hair.

Thea cried out again, and I held on. "That's it, baby. Come on ... push."

"He's coming!" I yelled out.

"Check ... the umbilical cord ... it's not around his neck."

"No!" I called out as Thea gasped.

"Okay, easy now, his shoulders—"

"He's coming!" Thea cried out and pushed one more time. I held my breath alongside of her. And the very next sound left me crying, as he cried out, screaming in her hands.

"Make sure nothing is in his nose or mouth, and don't cut the umbilical cord. Thea, keep him on your bare chest, and Levi get here as quick as possible. And happy new year."

I glanced back at the clock. 12:03 AM.

"Oh my God!" Thea cried as I helped bring her shirt down, tearing it a little bit. "Levi..."

"I know." I wiped my nose, and laughed as I got back in the driver's seat. I pulled off on the exit and drove toward the backroad.

"Hi ... hi..." Thea stroked him as he cried on her chest, cleaning his face with the ripped part of her shirt.

"He's here." I laughed again. I couldn't believe it. He was here. I wasn't sure what do but just laugh and drive.

It took us another seven minutes to get to the hospital. Once he got their Dr. Cohen, he stood a head taller than everyone else, as if his red hair didn't make him stick out enough. He was my sisters doctor and truthfully a workaholic, but it was a godsend since he always answered our calls.

Pulling to a stop in front, he and a bunch of nurses were ready. Wrapping Ulric in a blanket, double checking his mouth and nose, Dr. Cohen cut the cord, and the others carefully helped both Thea and Ulric out of the car, allowing me to breathe for the first time since ... since the bloody new year.

"We'll see you inside, Mr. Black!" Dr. Cohen called out to me, then focused on Thea as they wheeled her in on a stretcher.

Pressing the phone button once more, I made another call to the person I could count on to call everyone else.

"Levi, my boy. Happy New Year!"

"Dad ... he's here. And he's perfect."

BABY: DAY 45

THEA

I laughed, getting out of the hot tub as he reminded me of that day. "At least I don't have to worry about him not listening to me."

"How so?"

"I told him not to make me labor for hours. He listened."

"Do you mind telling him to go to sleep between the hours of nine and six like everyone else?" He laughed, and I rolled my eyes, and yawned.

He pulled out two gifts.

"Levi—"

"It's officially Valentine's Day, because someone spent her whole birthday hovering over our son."

"Someone sounds jealous..." I sang, skipping, yes skipping, over to him like I was a teenager and not a twenty-seven-year-old mother of one. Sitting next to him, I rested my chin on his shoulder.

"Happy Valentine's Day."

The first box … held my rings. He took out the pear-shaped diamond and slid it back to where it belongs on my ring finger.

"This kinda feels like a present for yourself," I teased, seeing as how he complained to high heaven I wasn't wearing my rings.

"So be it," he muttered, kissing my hand.

"The second, what? A marriage license?"

His eyes widened. "How did you know?"

"Levi—"

"Kidding." He laughed kissing my cheek and handed me the folder.

Opening, I stared at the company letterhead on the folder before opening. I sifted through the papers before looking up to him.

"When you come back to work, you can't come back empty handed, right?" He grinned at me and slowly as I began to realize the level of the case that was now in my hand, I began to grin as well.

"Seriously?"

"Everyone has been gunning for the chance to represent him. It's not a freebie. It's lunch with him and his agent. If you can sign him—"

"I'll be a total bad ass." I hugged it to my chest. "This is the best gift you've ever given me."

He frowned. "You mean, outside of my love, my son, a diamond ring, this tree house—"

"Yeah. Yeah!" I cut in, laughing, still hugging the folder. "Outside of the obvious."

He stared at me, waiting.

"What?"

"My gift."

I tried to be serious and stared back. "You mean, outside of already having my love, a son—"

"Yeah. Yeah. I saw you shove something into your purse before we left, so fork it over."

Rolling my eyes, I got up and moved to pick up my bag from the maze of clothes on the ground. Lifting the file, I handed it to him.

"You got me a case too?" He opened it, pulling out the papers. He stared at it for so long I was sure it would melt under the intensity of his gaze. Without a word, he flipped to the next page. And the next. And the next. Until he came to the end and started chuckling.

Looking over at me, he shook his head and pulled me into his lap. Coughing once to clear his throat, he flipped to the first page and held it in front of me.

"And this is?" he asked.

"I'm sure you can read it—"

"Say it."

Sighing, I nodded. "Application for our marriage license."

"And this?"

"Applications to get my new driver's license, social security card, passport. Also, my mail, insurance, doctor's notes, even voter registration."

"Why?"

He was really milking this; "Because my name is Thea Black, and no longer Thea Cunning."

"And this paper?"

"Levi!"

"Out with it."

"It's our new joint bank account," I answered.

He grinned like a mad man, and I put my hands on the side of his face and kissed him. Kissing his lips softly before everything just started to slip out of my mouth.

"I love you, Levi. The day you walked up to me in that bar was the first of many of the best days of my life. And nothing makes me happier, with the exception of our son, than knowing I get to spend the rest of my life with you … than knowing I'm your wife and you're my husband. So, happy Valentine's Day, baby. Sorry for taking so long."

He didn't say anything with his mouth, but his eyes spoke volumes. Flipping me on to my back on top of the bed, he rested his forehead against mine, his hand on my thigh.

"Mrs. Black," he whispered, kissing me.

"Yes."

"Mrs. Black." He kissed me again, and I answered.

"Yes."

Yes. I was Thea Black. Mother of Ulric Black. Wife of Levi Black. And damn proud of it.

PART TWO

PAST & PRESENT

PRESENT

LEVI

"Why do I have this annoying feeling you are trying to show off right now?" Tristan muttered as we rode up the elevator.

"I have no idea what you're talking about," I said. Tilting my hand even more to look at the tablet, so that it was the first thing anyone would see as we walked off the elevator.

"Good morning, Mr. Black. Mr. Knox," the receptionist said as we stopped in front of her. "Morning, Ms. Courtney. How has been the office been?" I asked, flexing my fingers as her blue eyes dropped to the ring, and then back to me quickly.

Smiling, she nodded. "Pretty much the same as always. I gave most of the details to Mr. Knox ... Congrats on your marriage, sir."

"Thank you." I nodded as I walked away. Within a few minutes, I was more than positive the whole firm would know. Ms. Courtney could get gossip through the office faster than wildfire. She was also good at getting gossip on other firms, which was why she was still here.

"Why am I friends with you?" Tristan snickered as we walked, nodding at the associates as we did.

"Welcome back, Mr. Black."

"Congratulations."

"It's good to see you, sir."

"Happy New Year."

All of their statements reminded me just how long it had been since I'd been in the office. I was a father now. A husband ... finally. By the time I made it to my corner office, I was actually tired of the welcome-back parade. However, Betty, being the old and sage woman she was, shot party streamers right at my face as soon as I stepped inside my fruit-basket-baby-gift-covered office. A large banner with the words WELCOME BACK hung on my window and blocked the view of my beautiful city.

"Welcome back, sir!" everyone yelled again, clapping.

"Jesus Christ." I jumped, glaring at Tristan, who clapped loudly in my ear. "Thank you. Thank you. Now, can someone please clean this shit up?"

It was like a maze getting to my desk. They all laughed, but one voice rang out louder than the rest.

"So unfair." I knew that voice. We all knew that voice.

Turning, they made way for her, as if she were splitting the Red Sea, my wife, Thea Black, dressed in a high-waisted black skirt and light pink blouse with a bow at the neck. She walked forward, into the middle of the department store that blew up in the middle of my office.

"I did all the heavy lifting, and you're the one who gets all the gifts." She picked up the giant teddy bear, and looked to the associates outside. "There wasn't even so much of a 'congrats' card on my desk."

"Thea!" Atticus Logan came up from the back, dressed in his black suit, though his jacket was off. His sandy blonde hair cut much shorter now. "I didn't realize you were coming back today."

"How else am I going to get my name on the wall?" she asked, setting the teddy bear back down.

In my most dead-serious tone, I reminded her, "I'm quite sure the name Black is up there."

"Then it either needs to be raised to the second power, or Black-Knox-Black will have to do," she shot back, just as seriously. And when I looked up at her, telling her not to push it here, on her first day, she just glared at me.

"You have a long, *long* way to go, *Mrs. Black*," Tristan spoke, walking up to my desk. "Before you become a name partner. Let's not get too ahead of ourselves."

She picked a pack of hazelnut tea out of the bag. "Do you mind if I take these? My clients are going to be here any moment."

"Clients?" Raymond, who was one of the oldest associates, AKA, the one who believed his name was going to get up on the wall, asked. "I wasn't aware you were working, Mrs. Black."

Tristan glanced at me. I stared at her. She smirked at all of us.

"Bullshit," I called her out.

"Betty." She turned to my secretary. "I'm surprised Mr. Black doesn't have the file already."

"I put it on his desk, and added it to his schedule along with his coffee mug." She nodded and walked toward the doors as everyone just stared.

Glancing under my palm, at said file, then at the coffee mug on the table, I pulled off the yellow sticky note. Cracking my jaw, I turned the note for Tristan to read. He glanced at it, and then back at her.

"The New England Patriots are your clients?!"

She frowned. "No!"

"Mrs. Black—"

"The wives of each of the New England Patriots are my clients, and we're going to sue the NFL." The frown on her face morphed into the most sinister grin as she held up the tea for me to see again. "Yes or no to the tea?"

Tristan looked to me, and I shook my head. The case I gave her was on the assault and battery of Mitchell Davey, running back for the New England Patriots. It was almost impossible to get the spouses of athletes to sue ... and yet somehow...

"Mrs. Black," Betty came over the intercom.

"Yes, Betty?" She called out, reaching for a tin of baskets to take with her as well.

"They're here."

Her eyes widened as she turned to me. "I'll be taking these; I've already set up a live stream in the conference room, as they prefer to have no men in the meeting. Welcome back, Boss."

She nodded, and headed out. The first person to speak was Tristan.

"So this is what it is like to have a good associate. It's been so long." Tristan sighed. "Meanwhile, this lot is just standing around, giving out teddy bears."

"Which dead weight are we letting go of first?" I asked, sitting back in my chair. In a flash, they were gone. It happened so quickly, the door didn't even have time to fully close. But when it did, Tristan spun to face me.

"You got married yesterday!" he snapped. "I know ... I was there! And you didn't think to let me know—"

"I didn't even know!" I snapped back, rubbing the side of my head as I lifted the case file. "She was just supposed to get Mrs. Davey to sue and now we're..."

I read the suit she planned to file, my mouth dropping open.

"What?" He waited impatiently

"Now we're the sons of bitches suing the NFL for Gross Negligence and Willful Misconduct toward the spouses of the players."

"On what grounds?!"

I couldn't help but laugh, because it was genius and very possible, so I read what was before me: "In 2013, the National Football League settled class action Concussion Litigations, which over the next 65 years, will cost the NFL $900 million, if not more. In so doing, the National Football League publicly brought attention to the detrimental impact that repeated blows had to the human brain and overall behavioral problems. And yet, since 2013, there has been no accountability for the second victims, the wives, many of whom were on the receiving end of their spouse's outbursts. Not only did the NFL fail in providing a guide to these women to care for their spouses, but repeatedly, they swept cases of domestic abuse under the rug. Other cases such as Mrs. Patricia Davey, who was beaten and dragged into a hotel room by her husband, Mitchell Davey, starting running back for the New England Patriots, was met with little to no attention by the mangers, head coaches, and other officials within the league. Mitchell Davey, who already has had two serious concussions, was suspended for only three games. First, he was told to work out his issues with his wife, with no guide to do so. Second, his wife was forced to deal with a hazardous situation, which she was not equipped to handle. Third, no further guidance or care was provided after said three-day suspension, despite being aware of the issues within their organization, the National Football League did and continues to do nothing."

When I looked up back at him, he was sinking into his seat, taking a deep breath. "We're going to have up security."

"Up security or 'round of the clock security," I muttered, putting the file on the desk. "Do you remember the last time lawyers tried to sue America's #1 sport? And that's when it was coming from former players." The backlash was swift and deep. Suing the NFL, for most people, was akin to suing football, and I knew people who loved football more than their own children.

"Your wife…" He shook his head. "You really didn't know?"

"No. And if she can hide this, I'm kinda terrified," I admitted. We'd just gotten married yesterday at The Ritz-Carlton, even though I couldn't remember anything other than her and our son. Not the décor, or the flowers my mother spent a fortune on, nor the beautiful view behind us. It was as if we were already married and just renewing vows, my attention was only on her.

PAST

LEVI

"She could still run." Tristan, the asshole, muttered behind me.

"I doubt it." Rolling my eyes, I glanced at Ulric, who tried to fit his fist into his mouth as my mother held him in her lap. She fixed the red bowtie around his neck and pointed to me. He looked up at me and laughed, reaching out for me.

"Levi."

"He's part of the wedding, too," I said, lifting him up and walking back on to the altar.

Tristan shook his head at me, but took a step back, making room for both of us. No sooner had I gotten back into place, the doors opened, and Vivian, walked out first in a silk red gown, holding on to white roses. Behind her was my sister, her eyes only on Tristan. Bellamy came out in her pink dress, tossing rose petals, and concentrating very hard at it, too. Tristan smiled, and pulled out his phone, taking more than a dozen photos at least.

113

Finally, she walked out, linking arms with her father on her right and her sister on her left. The star, my star, walked out gracefully, the long, white silk dress she wore was simple, not distracting anyone from the real beauty that was her. She held pink and red roses in her hands, laughing when she saw both Ulric and I waiting at the end for her.

"Slick move." Selene pouted, poking Ulric's cheek before moving.

"I had a threat a prepared for you, but seeing you hold my grandson made me forget it." Ben frowned at me, but put his hand on my shoulder, and stepped over for Thea to stand in front of me.

"Holding our son hostage?" Thea grinned, reaching out to cup his face.

"He reached out for me." I shifted over to one side. "Apparently, he also wanted to watch the most beautiful in the woman walk toward him."

She shook her head and laughed, reaching out to take my hand. "Always the smooth operator, Mr. Black."

I winked at her. "You haven't seen anything yet, Mrs. Black."

PRESENT

LEVI

"Earth to Levi!" Tristan snapped at me.

Glaring at him for cutting off my daydream, I hollered, "What?"

He nodded to the folder in front of me. "You know this will snowball; she can't take this case alone ... the whole firm is going to have to work it."

"Let her have the victory today. We'll talk—"

"We'll or you."

"I go alone, and she might pull a fast one on me, and next thing we know, we'll be Black-Knox-Black."

"And here I thought you always win—"

"How often do you win against Bethan?"

He groaned, rubbing his temple. "Why did you marry our associate again?"

Ignoring him, I leaned back, and thought of how this was going to work when I felt my phone buzz. I read the message and showed it to him.

"I take it back. Why didn't you marry her sooner?" He grinned.

The ladies are telling me other wives, from different teams, want in. We're going to need all hands on deck.

"Levi, I have Michael Shortz, the director of the NFL on the line; apparently, you aren't answering your phone," Betty buzzed in. I checked my phone, and sure enough, he was blocked. *Thea.*

"It's the first day," I reminded them all, because apparently, I was the only one not prepared for the shit storm coming. The only reason why Shortz was calling was to settle. The reason why he was blocked on my phone was because Thea knew he'd call and didn't want a damn settlement. She was that many moves ahead of me.

I looked to Tristan as he pulled a coin from his pocket. "Seriously?"

"You have a better way of choosing."

I waved my hand for him to go on.

"Heads," I called when he flipped it into the air.

"Tails," he said, and I picked up the phone.

"Put him through, Betty," I replied.

"Mr. Black—"

"We aren't settling unless you admit guilt *and* pay out," I told him directly, and Tristan's brows rose.

"This will get very ugly, very quickly, Mr. Black. Do you know how many people love football in this country?"

I smirked. "Who do you think will play me in the next movie about the league? I still think *Concussion* was robbed during the Oscars."

Dial tone.

"What did he say?" Tristan asked when I hung up the phone.

"He said Chris Pine, and here I was thinking more Jake Gyllenhaal or maybe Aidan Turner?"

"What?"

"The movie version of me." I laughed, taking the baseball from my desk and leaning backward.

He stood up; "You're a twat."

"A twat?" I laughed.

"Yes." He nodded, walking toward the door. "Now excuse me as I go prepare for the biggest case we'll have this year, if ever … you know the one your wife got … not you. She deserves to play herself … with Jake Gyllenhaal… *or maybe Aidan Turner.*"

I bit my tongue to keep from cursing him out as he left. He just had to piss in my cheerios. Breathing in, I ignored him, typing on my phone quickly to ask if she got permission for me to view the feed.

I did.

Nodding, I sat up and lifted my laptop open when she texted again.

My welcome back gift was so much better than theirs.

Smirking, I replied, *We'll see.*

Tristan didn't seem to get that Thea and I were a team. Her wins were my wins. Her cases, my cases and vice versa. There was going to be no grace period when we turned. No natural end to a happily ever after, because we just kept moving forward. There was always something more. And this next battle, I couldn't wait to fight it with her.

I didn't want to settle either.

I'd always wanted to behead a Goliath.

Like she'd said, she and I were going to make waves together.

PART THREE

THE FUTURE & FURTHER INTO THE FUTURE

THE FUTURE

THEA

He'd been upset for the whole weekend, but had just kept it bottled up until now. He looked back at me, and I nodded. Taking a deep breath, he stood straighter, and, holding a piece of paper in his hands, he knocked.

"Come in."

Tiptoeing to the door with the sippy cup top I'd just finished washing, I cracked the door a little more to hear. Levi glanced up from his desk, his glasses low on his nose.

"Ulric? What is it?"

Again, Ulric turned back to me, and I winked at him. He turned to his father and lifted the paper to read. Levi glanced at me, and I tried not smile, but I couldn't help it. He rose from his desk, and walked around to our son.

"I, Ulric Pierre-Od ... Oid-ss—"

"O-id-hche." Levi helped him pronounce, still confused as to what was happening but patient, nonetheless.

"I, Ulric Pierre-Oidche-Black, am quitting baseball..."

"What?"

"Levi," I hissed out his name, and he glared at me so I glared right back. We battled through our eyes until he finally looked back down at our son.

"Go on."

"I, Ulric Pierre-Oidche-Black, am quitting baseball ... not because it is hard. But because ... because..." He sighed. "Because everyone sucks, Dad."

"Ulric!" I stomped into the room.

"It's true! I'm the MVP, but why do I have to do everything?"

Levi released a breath of relief, dropping to eye level with our seven-year-old MVP of the Boston Beagles Little League.

"Kiddo, I know you are upset about losing the championships, but remember, it's a team sport. You can't let your teammates down."

He groaned. "But they let me down."

"So you want to quit? That's not what sports are about, son."

"No ... ugh." He scratched his curls and lifted the paper again to read. "I'm not quitting because it is hard, but because I want to play tennis. And I promise not to quit again."

"Tennis?" Levi looked at him like he was an alien.

But Ulric grinned, happily nodding his head. "If I play tennis, I still get to be on a team, but each game is just me and somebody else. It's like what you and Mommy say Willow and I have to do."

"Share?" Levi asked, still frowning.

Ulric shook his head. "No, co-promise."

"Compromise," Levi corrected.

Ulric nodded. "Yeah! There is a team I can join. And I want to learn. I just want to play by myself! Then, if I win or lose, it's my fault."

Levi looked to me, as if he were begging for help.

I shrugged, unsure what to tell him.

"Sorry, Dad." Ulric's shoulders dropped, and he hung his head. "I know you like baseball, and I like it, but I don't wanna play. I mean, I'll still play with you if you want."

My heart felt like it was hit by a truck. Levi, heartbreakingly put his hands on his head, running them through his curls. "It's okay. Thank you for telling me. I'll talk to the coach. Then we can look into this tennis stuff."

"Really? Thanks, Dad." Ulric hugged him, and then made a run for it right past me.

"No running in the house!" I yelled after him. "And check on your sister!"

"I blame you," Levi muttered, picking up Ulric's written declaration. He frowned at it, as if it were a dead animal. "I knew you'd poison him against the game."

"Hey!" I pointed Willow's sippy cup top at him. "You heard him ... he doesn't want to carry the team anymore. He was so crushed on Saturday. He cried in the car while the other kids were drinking juice boxes in the shade."

"If the other kids' parents would have taught their kids how to catch a damn ball. Or at least run down everything—"

"Levi, they are seven. Ulric is the weird one," I reminded him, laughing.

"Hey!" He pointed back at me. "Ulric, isn't weird; he's dedicated to—"

"Winning. He loves winning," I reminded him, walking farther into the study.

"So? He's not a jerk about it."

I made a face. Ulric said the same thing when I told him he loved to win too much. 'I'm not being mean to them about it, Mommy.' And he's exactly right. He can't play with the older kids because he isn't big enough. He doesn't feel like everyone is working hard like him. And when he loses, he can't blame himself because he thinks he did everything he could, and everyone else let him down. He's right. So instead of yelling at everyone, and being a little monster, our son wants to play a sport where he can only blame himself if he loses. This is good."

He still pouted, dropping the paper on his desk and leaning back against it. "I know nothing about tennis."

"You can learn together."

"Or I can find him an All-Star seven-year-old team." He thought about it, and I smacked his shoulder.

"Let him at least play tennis. You never know ... he could end up hating it and missing baseball."

He sighed, and reached out, putting his hands on my hips. "Promise me he'll hate it."

"You are ridiculous!" I wiggled away from him and back toward the door. "Now, come on and help me. Willow's friends will be here soon."

"How is she two already?" he muttered to himself as we walked to the living room. Willow sat on the floor, her curly hair in two big pigtails as Ulric gave her all his baseball stuff.

"Ulric, what are you doing?" Levi asked.

"I'm giving Willow her birthday gifts," he replied happily, rubbing salt deep into Levi's open, bleeding wounds.

"It looks like you're trying to get rid of your old stuff by giving it to your sister." I crossed my arms and eyed him up.

"No, she likes this stuff." He grinned, still trying to weasel his way out of it. Before I could get a word in, Willow threw the ball right at my head. I ducked, even though Levi caught the ball. She started to giggle, and then looked for something else to throw.

"Willow!" I pointed at her as she picked up the mitt and threw it. For how heavy it was for her, she threw it pretty far.

"Look whose got Daddy's arm." Levi grinned, rushing to her, and scooped her off the ground, causing her to laugh harder. When she laughed, her smile took up her whole face, and her eyes squinted together hiding her beautiful hazel eyes.

"Don't cheer her on," I warned him, walking up to them. "No throwing."

"Ulric, take all of your stuff back upstairs."

"It's her stuff."

"Ulric." I stared him down.

"Yes, Mommy," he grumbled, picking the items up one by one.

"And you." I pointed to Levi, who stared at my finger, then back at my eyes. "Don't you go trying to replace Willow for Ulric in baseball."

He grinned, just as sneaky as his son. "Just for a little bit, and watch, he'll want to play with us too. Right, Willow, right?"

"And if they both hate it…"

He made a face at me. "Seriously? Why not just rip out my heart already?"

"No throwing in the house." I pointed to them both as I headed to the kitchen.

"How long you think your big brother will play tennis? Huh? He'll come back when we start to play. *Willow*, you're *so* smart," I heard him say after I walked away.

Rolling my eyes, I did my best ignore him.

FURTHER INTO THE FUTURE

LEVI

"Why is it so hot?" she complained, looking into her purse. "Have any of you seen my fan?"

I glanced to the right, as our daughter popped the bubble gum in her mouth, staring at me. The fan buzzed in her hand. She leaned back, trying to hide behind my body. Snickering to myself, I leaned forward some.

"Nope," I answered my wife.

"So weird … I thought I…" Thea trailed off as she glanced at me.

"Yeah."

"I thought I told Willow to throw it in here for me." She moved to see her, but I leaned to block her view.

"Really?"

"Willow!"

"Mom, my face is melting!" Willow whined when Thea shoved me, reaching over for the fan.

"Whose fault is that I told you to buy one at the gift shop? But no, you wanted that shirt, so fork it over." Thea wiggled her fingers, waiting.

Willow looked to me, holding the fan to her chest with a pout on her face. Her big hazel eyes teared up. "Daddy, help—"

"Don't you dare," Thea snapped at me.

Taking a deep breath, I leaned back, allowing them to fight it out on their own. "This is why he didn't want us to come."

"Excuse me—"

"Ladies and gentlemen, on Centre Court," the announcer cut in, "competing in his first ever Wimbledon, Ulric Pierre-Oidhche Black."

Everyone clapped. I, on the other hand, stood up and cheered him as he came out.

"DAD!" Willow hissed.

"LEVI!" Thea pulled on my jeans.

Ignoring them both, I pointed to him.

He pulled his hat down more, but raised a small fist for me, causing a few people to laugh.

"Sit down!" Thea yanked, and I finally did, grinning from ear to ear. "This isn't baseball. You can't be hollering like that."

"Thea." I smiled at her. "Our son is playing in Wimbledon."

She melted, her grin spreading. She put her hands to the side of her face and yelled, "I love you, sweetheart!"

I laughed, as he covered his face with both hands.

"O-M-G. You guys are so not cool," Willow groaned, trying to hid her face.

"We know," we said simultaneously. We happily gave up on being cool nineteen years ago. Looking back on it ... it was the best choice we'd even made.

Sneak Peek at CHILDREN OF VICE

Reader Discretion Advised

VICE
noun \\ˈvīs
a : moral depravity or corruption : WICKEDNESS
b : a physical imperfection, deformity, or taint
c : an abnormal behavior pattern in a domestic animal detrimental to its health or usefulness

PROLOGUE

"Monsters make choices.
Monsters shape the world.
Monsters force us to become stronger, smarter, better.
They sift the weak from the strong and provide a forge for the steeling of
souls. Even as we curse monsters, we admire them. Seek to become them,
in some ways. There are far, far worse things to be than a monster."
~ Jim Butcher

ETHAN

I'm not sure when it happened...

When it began to crack and alter shape...

Looking back, there are so many moments that could be the one, the origin.

If you asked anyone who wasn't family, they'd say it happened the day I was born.

That the moment I came into this world as a Callahan, the innocence, the morality, and the virtues that are normally common to everyone else were defective. Like a house with fractured windows. If you asked anyone within my family they'd say the windows were not fractured, but frosted and bulletproof because that is how they should be. After all, the people who were pointing at my windows were the same people who used blinds. That was my family all right...stupidly rich, dangerously powerful, unspeakably ruthless, and obsessed with extended metaphors. But the thing was...I didn't care if I was a house with fractured or frosted or bulletproof windows. If people were curious to know the type of man I was, they were free to find out at their own peril.

What I cared about was when.

When did it happen?

When did I understand what it meant to be a Callahan?

To be Ethan Antonio Giovanni Callahan.

Staring up at the waters above me until my eyes drifted closed, one memory, one moment came forward...

ETHAN - AGE ELEVEN

He looked like what everyone said Santa Claus was supposed to look like...with everything but the long white beard, though, which made his red faced, white fat body, cloaked in red robes disturbing to see.

"Why is there a screen here if I can still see you?"

He laughed. "Is this your first confession, boy?"

I don't like hi,. I thought immediately and for three good reasons too.

One, he laughed when I was being serious.

Two, he didn't answer my question.

Three, he called me "boy."

"Yes," I answered anyway but only because Mom told me to be respectful in church.

"By your seat there is a card. It will tell you what you have to say."

I really don't like him.

Why would you put a card in a dark stall? It was stupid.

Reaching around me, I got the small little card and lifted it up, reading.

"Forgive me, Father, for I have sinned...but no, I haven't." I looked back up at him.

"*Really now?*" he said, his voice going up. "You haven't done anything wrong?"

"Nope."

"Sometimes we may think things aren't wrong or so small that they aren't sins, but God cares about them all," he replied.

"Okay, when I have something, I'll come back," I told him, putting the card down.

"So you've never said anything to hurt someone? Maybe pushed your little sister—"

"Why would I push my sister?"

"Or hit your brother?"

"Didn't do that either."

"Yelled or fought with your parents?"

"No. My parents would kill me and then bring me back to kick my ass to Ireland so every Callahan there could kill me again." I laughed at that. I liked Ireland. Everyone was kinda like Uncle Neal.

"Callahan?"

The way he said the name made me pay attention to him. He said it like…like it was shocking or scary even. No. When I looked into his blue eyes they were wide-open and shaking. I didn't know that was possible. Maybe his whole head was shaking and I could only really see his eyes.

"Yeah." I nodded, adding, "I'm Ethan Antonio Giovanni Callahan, first son of Liam Alec Callahan and Melody Nicci Giovanni Callahan. Are you new to this church?"

He didn't reply, so I knocked on the screen.

"Why are you scared?"

When I spoke, he sat up straighter and focused in on me. "I'm not scared."

"You're lying…you should confess that."

His whole jolly priest shtick went away when he spoke again. "Understanding who your parents are, I now see why you are so ill-mannered and pompous at such a young age."

Hurt him!

I wanted to, but I kept talking instead. "Who do you think my parents are? I'm sure—"

"It's not who I think they are. It's who they are. Murderers."

"So?" I asked him.

"So? So?"

I nodded. "Moses was a murderer. King David was a murderer. Actually almost everyone in the Bible is a murderer...except Jesus. But since he's part of God, doesn't that make him a murderer by connection? Because God tells people to kill people too and—"

His voice started to rise. "You are twisting God's words."

"No, it's there. I'm sure."

"You..." He took a deep breath. "In the Bible, boy, God is seeking justice, a righteousness for the whole world, in a world in which there are bad people who hurt people, because back then there were no jails. There was no way to stop people from continuing to hurt and cheat others. The church teaches us that every life is precious and in a modern world, jails do exist. As such murder is a sin."

"What about the army?"

"It is for the overall wellbeing of the country and only approved by the church if it is absolutely necessary."

Are all adults dumb like this?

"So then being a murderer is okay. You just need permission. And you can only get permission if it is necessary. My parents only do things if it is necessary—"

"Nothing your parents do, boy—"

"Stop interrupting me!" I snapped, glaring at him as I stood up in the booth. "Stop calling me boy. I told you my name is Ethan Antonio Giovanni Callahan. I haven't interrupted you once. I've allowed you to speak your mind. And you're the one being rude. I told you they are my parents and you still want to talk bad about them to me. If gossiping isn't a sin, it should be and you should confess to it. My parents only act if it is necessary. People attack us all the time, and we defend ourselves, our families, and our people. If my parents weren't murderers…if I wasn't a murderer. We'd be dead!"

He gasped. "What did you just say?"

I didn't reply. The more I looked at him, the angrier I got.

"You've killed someone?"

"Yes, but I'm not asking for forgiveness."

Again he made another huffy sound.

"What have they done to you? How old are you that they turned you into a monster?"

"Thanks be to God." I quoted the last line from the confession card he'd told me to pick up before, which meant we were done. Opening the door, I blinked a few times, adjusting to the light.

"Ethan, what took so long?" Dona popped up right in my face. Her dark brown hair was curled up a lot and it made her look funny, but she still liked it. She was grinning like she knew something I didn't. Dona's smile always made me smile no matter what, though.

But before I could say anything, she was already heading toward the booth I'd just exited.

Grabbing her arm, I pulled her back. "Don't go to him."

She looked at me for a long time before nodding and stepping back next to me. "All the other ones are full. Daddy, Mommy, and Wyatt went in."

I looked around the cathedral and in the wooden rows were all of Mom and Dad's people. Two were directly behind Dona, speaking to each other, and a few others moved through the crowd to be closer to one of the stalls where I guessed Dad, Mom, or Wyatt were.

"Just wait for another one."

"Okay," she agreed, sliding into one of the rows, her green dress puffing up when she did.

Just when I sat down next to her to wait, another person moved to the stall, but jerk face Santa Claus came out. He didn't look at me. Well, I think he couldn't see me over all the other people. He apologized to the guy trying to go in next. For some reason I couldn't look away. I had this feeling in me and I didn't know what it was.

"Where are you going?"

I didn't realize I was standing and moving until Dona spoke.

"To the bathroom," I lied and started to walk through the crowd.

"Ethan!" one of my dad's guards called out to me.

"Bathroom!" I lifted my phone for him to see. I knew he was still following me, but I didn't care. I wasn't doing anything bad. Plus, all the people made it hard for him to catch up.

When I made it out of the main chapel, I looked to my left and right, but the fatso was gone. I went right because…well, why would he go to the church gift shop? The farther down the hall I went, the darker it became, and the light coming in from the blue stained glass made it look like the sky before it rained. I walked and walked until I got to a hall with a sign that said 'priests only.' Ignoring it, I walked down the hall. Most of the doors were closed, but one was cracked open the tinniest bit. I heard his voice.

"What do you mean the audio did not work?"

Tilting my head and looking through the slit, the fatso stood near the glass window, trying to look out at someone, gripping the phone in his hand.

"Fine. Fine. That doesn't matter. The boy confessed it. I heard him say with his own mouth that he and his parents were murderers."

What?

It was only then did I notice the wires on his desk.

It clicked.

He was new.

He was new and came to this church, my parents' church, hating my parents.

"So you're saying even if I testify it's not enough? What do you want me to do? Catch them in the act?" he yelled so loudly I guessed he didn't hear the door as I came in.

But then again it was even quieter than I thought it was.

"Look, the deal was…no, you listen to me! The deal was I do this and no one finds out about Ohio. I will not—ugh—ahh!"

"—ugh—ahh!" Those were the sounds he made as my knife went into his back.

Thump.

The phone slipped out of his hands as he tried to turn. I pulled the knife from his back and I watched as his red robe got darker and darker as the blood left his body.

"What…what…what did you…?"

"This." I stabbed him over and over again, anywhere I could, his huge body falling backward, trying to grab onto the desk but crashing to the floor.

"Aww, man!" I groaned at my now broken knife. "I just got this one too!"

Sighing, annoyed, I picked up the phone, which already disconnected. Stepping over him, I grabbed the wires and pulled and cut them.

"Mon…mon…"

"Monday?" I turned back to him.

He was trying to crawl, but to where I didn't know. "Mon…"

"Monkey?"

His belly rose and fell, rose and fell. He was in shock, I think. He was staring at me in shock. His blue eyes shone with tears, not sad tears. Or forgive me tears. Just another liquid coming out of his body.

"Monster," I said to him. "That's what you want to call me, right? This week in school they made us read *Frankenstein*. It was cool. I liked it. I like books that make me think. That's why I'm in the advanced class. My favorite part is when the monster looks at Dr. Frankenstein and tells him it's his fault. It kinda reminds me of now. You called me a monster. I walked away. Then you threatened the monster. And so if it comes down to you or me, I have to pick me."

"Go to—"

Taking out my second knife…well, Wyatt's knife, I stabbed him in the throat and pulled it out quickly. When I did, blood went everywhere. Wiping my face, I walked to the stained glass window, trying to see what he was looking at before.

"Ethan?"

Turning around, I saw it was my dad's guard. He looked between me and the guy in red…I wasn't sure if he was a cop or priest. Pulling out his phone, he dialed one number before speaking.

"Dozen Lilies delivered to my location," he said, walking closer to us.

"From Ethan," I added.

He just stared at me, and so I stared back.

"Yes, that's right. A dozen lilies from…the second. Let the boss know."

"Let them all know," I whispered mostly to myself, staring at both of the knives in my hands.

Rule 103: always have a knife.

Discover More by J.J. McAvoy

Ruthless People Series
Ruthless People
The Untouchables
American Savages
A Bloody Kingdom
Declan + Coraline (a prequel novella)

Children of Vice Series (the children of Ruthless People)
Children of Vice

Single Title Romances
Black Rainbow
Rainbows Ever After (an after-the-happily-ever-after novella)
Sugar Baby Beautiful
Child Star
That Thing Between Eli and Gwen

About the Author

J.J. McAvoy was born in Montreal, Canada and graduated from Carleton University in 2016 with an honours degree in Humanities. She is the oldest of three and has loved writing for years. Her works are inspired by everything from Shakespearean tragedies to modern pop culture. Her first novel, Ruthless People, was a runaway bestseller. Currently she's traveling all across the world, writing, looking for inspiration, and meeting fans. To get in touch, please stay in contact via her social media pages, which she updates regularly.

https://www.facebook.com/iamjjmcavoy/
https://twitter.com/JJMcAvoy

Made in the USA
Middletown, DE
27 April 2023

29570745R00086